12-19-2019

To my comic relief 😊

May our work days be
Short,
Our laughs be long,
And our memories together
be plentiful...
Here's to our future 😊

To Light

SMOTHERED

JO LIGHT

ISBN: 978-1-54399-337-0 (print)
ISBN: 978-1-54399-338-7 (ebook)

"All of us, whoever we may be, have our respirable beings.
We lack air and we stifle. Then we die.
To die for lack of love is horrible.
Suffocation of the soul."

-Victor Hugo, *Les Miserables*

CHAPTER ONE

THE NIGHT WAS RAW. THE ICY HANDS OF WINTER'S GRIP, desperate to squeeze the remaining life from the fall season, grew stronger with each passing day. It had been raining for a few hours and a steady stream water of ran along the sidewalks falling into the murky depths of the streets' storm drains. The sky was black, the moon covered by dark, gray clouds. No stars were visible through the immense cloud cover. Darkness enveloped him as he sat in his beat up black '86 Ford Taurus. The only sound was the rain pounding down. He watched the drops hit the windshield of the car, falling fast, obscuring the outside world into a blurry dream. The car was filled with the smell of stale cigarette smoke and the slight hint of body odor, but he didn't mind or didn't notice. His heartbeat was steady. His breath, deep and slow, billowed out before him in a vapor mist in the cold car. He had been sitting two houses down from her home for two hours now, watching. A single light glowed through the large bay window of the two-bedroom Cape that she had inherited from her grandmother when she had passed only days ago. He remembered reading the obituary and feeling a pang of sadness for her. He knew once the grandmother had died she would be all alone. She had no other family, no one to turn to. *Maybe she could turn to me*, he thought.

He sat up slightly, barely hearing the groan of the old leather seat beneath him as he shifted his weight. He was quite a large man and, at six-four and two hundred-fifty pounds, the car responded to the repercussions of his stirrings. He was very muscular from years of manual labor jobs he picked up here and there. He thought it quite funny when he looked at himself in the mirror, the way his muscles swelled under his skin. He was never supposed to be able to grow like that. The doctors had told his mother that he would always be small due to all of his medical problems. He had been born two months early. The doctors had told her it was from all the stress she had been under. She had almost died giving birth to him, and he had been born with a hole in his heart. He had spent a good part of his first three years in and out of the hospital enduring extensive surgeries. His mother had been by his side constantly. His father, on the other hand, had never once shown his ugly mug at the hospital - not even when he was born, not once. He hated the fact that he looked just like him. He had his hair, his face, and even his temper. As if on cue, a tidal wave of anger crashed through him at the mere thought of his father. *Stop it,* he told himself. *You are here for her, not to think about him.* He took a few deep breaths and held them, then counted to ten. When his anger had subsided he laid back a little, sinking into the seat and rubbing his temples. He wasn't happy that it was raining. It made it hard for him to watch her.

He reached over to the passenger seat and pulled out a Camel cigarette. He was just about to light it when he saw her at the window. His heartbeat quickened and his breath caught in his throat. It was difficult to see clearly, but he knew it was her.

"Damn car windows… Damn rain…. Damn it!" he growled.

The windows were fogging up and the rain pounded harder, making her look as if she were inside a waterfall. He couldn't risk turning on the car defrost or the windshield wipers for fear that he might be seen by someone. He was taking a big chance sitting here this late at night on a street as quiet as this one. This was the fifth time he had come here to watch her in the last two months, and his fear of being caught was just as strong tonight as it had been the very first night.

Her home was in a cul-de-sac in a family neighborhood with many small tract homes lined up neatly and built very close together. They were all small Cape-style homes painted in different colors with yards that were each set up a little differently. They all had the same layout with either two or three bedrooms. He figured any unknown car sitting out in the street at two in the morning might raise some suspicions in a neighborhood like this. However, hers was the only light on at this hour.

She moved slowly toward the bay window and stood for a while. The glow from the lamp behind her cast an eerie glow around her. He thought she must look like an angel in what he imagined to be a white nightgown. He figured, if he could get a closer look, it was probably slightly sheer. He hoped she was not wearing a bra or any underwear. His lower lip quivered slightly. Even though he couldn't see her face through the rain and fogged up windows, he could picture every detail of her. Her hair was long and brown with the slightest hints of red and gold. When she left it loose, it fell a few inches past her shoulders. She usually wore it in a long braid or pulled back in a bun off her neck. *Oh her neck*, he shivered as he thought of her long sleek neck delineated by the beautiful curve of her face. Her cheekbones were set high and her nose was perfect, unlike his misshapen, slightly flattened one. She had olive skin that turned a beautiful toasted almond during the summer months. Her breasts were not large, but they were not small.

When he saw her in the mornings, he could sometimes spy her nipples through her sports bra and tank top.

He remembered the first time he had seen her. It had been towards the end of summer last year. Even though it had been six in the morning it was already extremely hot. It was one of the last days in August, a day that the weather-man promised was going to be complete with sweltering heat and humidity. You know, the one he liked to call "a good ole' Triple H today, folks." The kind of day when you can't buy an ice cream without it melting on you within minutes. He had been just about to leave the cafe as she walked in, slightly out of breath. He remembered glancing up at her and thinking that he might know her from somewhere. A feeling of recognition flowed through him. Her skin had been so brown that day, glazed with sweat. Her arms and legs were toned and her muscles rippled from exhaustion.

She smiled brilliantly at the girl behind the counter when the friendly barista asked her "the usual?" A few minutes later the girl smiled back at her and said "Here ya go, Alex," and handed her a jar of the cafe's well known homemade jelly along with an iced coffee. That was when he realized who she was. He had just seen her in the Daily News the day before. *Alexandra something...what was her last name?* He couldn't remember at the time. He had read that she was being recognized by the Homicide Unit of the Newbury Police Department. She had helped solve a murder case they had been working on by profiling the murder suspect - some serial killer that had racked up five kills. The article claimed she had some kind of degree in psychology. He recalled being impressed with her beauty, quite visible in the picture from the paper. But there, up close and in person, he was blown away. As she turned to grab a napkin, she bumped into him. He hadn't known she was so close to him. He had been trying to slide past her to leave. She looked up at him and apologized. Her eyes seared him, freezing him in place, stealing any words or sense of reasoning from him. He felt a tingle in his upper thighs as a streak of lightning heat flew from his chest down to his groin. Her eyes were almond shaped with thick black eyelashes that any woman would pay big money to have. But the color, the color was what held him in a trance. They were the bluest of blue with flecks of green and yellow strewn throughout and a dark blue ring encircling them. From that moment on her eyes haunted his dreams at night.

He watched her now at the window. For a split second he thought she might be looking straight at him. He slumped down in the seat of the car as fast as he could. *Did she see me?* He could have sworn she had looked straight at him. He could almost feel the pressure from her eyes boring a hole right through his body. But his fear was quickly replaced with relief as she moved away from the window. In the next few minutes the light in the living room was gone and he was staring at the window, black and empty. Within seconds he was missing her.

He sat another ten minutes alone on the quiet street. Still the only sound he could hear was the rain pounding on his car and his heartbeat, which had finally slowed once again. He wiped a few beads of sweat from his forehead and took a very deep breath. He held it, just like he used to do as a kid, until he felt a tingling in his scalp like little black ants climbing all over his brain. He waited until the lightheaded feeling almost took complete control and then let the air out, breath bursting from his lips.

The thought of doing it tonight crossed his mind, the images overwhelming. Could he? Was he ready? *No, not yet.* He hadn't had enough time with her yet - observing her, watching her, wanting her. No, now was not the time. He needed more time to think. He put the keys in the ignition and started the car. He let the car crawl slowly down the suburban street without turning on his headlights. He waited until he was all the way to the end of her road before doing so. The lights pierced through the rain, the raindrops reflecting them like little teardrops dancing in a spotlight, shimmering. He could not chance being seen. Not when he was this close. Not when he had been so patient and had waited so long……..

CHAPTER TWO

THE MORNING LIGHT FILTERED IN THROUGH ALEX Aguilar's bedroom window. Little rays of sunlight bounced all around her as she slowly opened her eyes. She blinked a few times, trying to pull herself out of the hazy cloud of sleep. *At least the rain has passed*, she thought. She lay there a moment contemplating whether she wanted to get up or not. She was tired and drained of all her energy. Sleep had been eluding her since her grandmother passed away. It had only been a few days since she had buried her, and the deep empty pit in her stomach seemed to feel just as vacant today as it had the day her Abuela died. She knew it was inevitable. Abuela had lived a long time, and Alex knew she couldn't live forever.

"Eighty-eight years on this great earth is enough for me, mija. Mi tiempo ha pasado - my time has passed," Abuela had said to her. Hearing that hadn't made Alex feel any better about it, even though now her grandmother's pain was gone.

Her grandmother had been diagnosed with ovarian cancer just six months prior to her death. She was a strong woman before the cancer had taken her. Even in her late eighties she was very mobile, and her mind was as quick as a priest's liturgy on Super Bowl Sunday. That is what bothered Alex the most, having to watch her grandmother wilting away, wasting away, dying. Her grandmother had been a staunch Catholic - raised in the Catholic Church since birth. She was not afraid of death. To her death was just a passing, a way to cielo - to heaven. Her Mexican ancestors had taught her that the body dies but the soul rises up. Abuela had not been afraid because she knew all her other loved ones were in heaven waiting for her. The only thing she had been concerned about was Alex.

Alex had come to live with Abuela when she was nine. Her parents had died tragically in a car accident, and her only living relative was her grandmother. Abuela became her mother, her father, and her grandmother all at once. But most of all, over the years they had been together, Abuela had become her best friend. That is why Abuela had worried so much about her. Since the death of her parents, Abuela had watched Alex fold into herself, shunning away from friendships, relationships, and, ultimately, love. Once Abuela was gone, Alex would be completely alone. Abuela tried to get Alex to go out, to enjoy life, to open up to someone. It seemed the more she pushed, the more Alex poured herself into her work. In the last few years, her grandmother had started to really worry. She hadn't ever wanted to leave Alex to a lonely, loveless, solitary life. On Abuela's deathbed Alex had promised to try and get out, to find friends, to find a relationship, to find love. Now, thinking back, Alex wished she had never even mouthed the words. She lay there for a moment thinking of the words she had spoken, remembering the look of happiness that had spread across her grandmother's face, then the emptiness in her eyes that had followed. It had been as if that was the only thing holding her back from her journey to the other side - making sure Alex was going to be okay.

A soft purring came from beneath the covers, yanking Alex from her memories. She smiled, for a moment forgetting the sadness that had been close to crushing her chest. Elefantito moved beneath the covers just slightly, demanding attention. The gray tiger cat had been with her for nearly six years. Abuela had named her Elefantito (baby elephant in Spanish) because, for such a small cat, she was very loud when she roamed the house. Now she was the only thing Alex had left. The cat moved again, poking her head from beneath the blanket to look at Alex.

When Alex found her she had been just a kitten weighing only two pounds. Alex had been on her morning run one very cold November morning and stopped when she heard a loud cry coming from the top of a maple tree. She looked up to find a tiny kitten shivering and scared. Alex climbed the tree to free her new furry friend. She still remembered the look on Abuela's face as she walked into the house cuddling the tiny creature. Abuela loved all the creatures of the earth, but she wasn't fond of having them roam through her immaculately clean home.

"Que es esto? What on earth do you have there, mija?" she had asked, one eyebrow raised. Alex knew she was in for a discussion. She sucked in a deep breath.

"I found it stuck in a tree. I think it is lost. Look how thin it is...." Her eyes, pleading, looked straight into Abuela's.

"And what are you planning to do with it, mija?" Abuela asked, one eyebrow still raised, but with a slight upward tilt of her lips.

"I was hoping we could keep it" Alex said quietly. The kitten began to purr at that moment, warm and content, cradled in Alex's arms.

Abuela looked at Alex, looked at the kitten, and then back at Alex and said, "You had better clean up after it, mija." Then she turned and walked out of the room with a sigh. Alex had known her grandmother wouldn't say no.

Alex scratched lightly under the cat's chin while she considered taking her morning run. She usually ran four miles every morning to wake up and to clear her head. Since her grandmother had died, she hadn't stepped foot outside of the house other than to go to the funeral. She had taken a few days off from work, canceling quite a few patients unfortunately. Right now her office was the last thing on her mind. She thought about calling Manny, her dearest and only real friend. He had been her rock during these last few days.

She had met Manuel Castillo in college. He had been in many of her criminal justice classes. She was taking a course in "Criminal Minds" as part of her degree in psychology, and he was studying the same for the police department. He was quite handsome; very tall with dark brown hair and hazel eyes that seemed to imprint on the brain. Still, Alex had kept her distance. She wasn't there to find a boyfriend. She was there to get an education, to prepare for a career. Manny tried asking her out a few times in the beginning, but she politely declined. Eventually, he gave up on asking her out and asked if they could at least be friends. Alex wasn't interested in finding any friends either, but figured she could use a study partner. They began studying together and wound up becoming very close friends after all. Manny was the only friend, besides Abuela, that Alex had.

In the first few weeks of getting to know each other they realized that they were from the same area, growing up only twenty miles apart. They found it funny that they attended rival high schools and may have even been at some of the same high school football games. Alex remembered secretly thinking it was because she never would have talked to him, or anyone, before then. She was too embarrassed to admit she had never shown her face at any extracurricular activities or been involved in anything other than her studies. She had really closed herself off after her parents passed. Alex had never allowed herself any kind of friendship through middle and high school due to her deep seated fear of loss. She was quite surprised at herself for being so open to a new friendship all of a sudden, especially with a handsome single guy. There was just something about him. Even though she had just met Manny, she felt as if she had known him for years.

Following college they both returned to their respective home-towns. After a few years of working at a clinic to gain experience, Alex opened up an office in the city. Manny went to work for the local police department and soon worked his way up the ranks. She had to laugh about it. If she hadn't known he had been from the area, she would have thought he was following her around when he told her he would be working in the same town. She sighed a little. It was hard to believe that was ten years ago. Now they worked together on homicide cases, she with her knowledge in Psychology and he, conducting his detective work. He had risen to Lead Detective quickly, which never surprised Alex. She knew he would. He was a hard worker. She smiled as she thought of him and how seriously he took his work.

Alex slowly stood from the bed, trying not to startle Elefantito. Still, with the movement, Elefantito bolted off the bed and ran to one of his many hiding places. Alex chuckled a little at the cat's startled reaction. She walked over to her bedroom window and looked out for a few minutes. The sun warmed her face and bare shoulders. She stared up towards the sky. It was hard to tell that it had rained last night. Except for the small puddles of water that still remained on the back porch and the glistening leaves on the trees, there was no sign of rain. The rich blue palate of sky was sprinkled lightly with white, puffy clouds. The sun gleamed. She whispered good morning to the heavens, hoping Abuela could hear her. A single tear ran down her cheek, and she brushed it away with the back of her hand. She had decided last night that she had mourned enough. Abuela would not have approved of her sulking around.

She moved over to the edge of her bed and sat down. She pulled her nightgown up and over her head, feeling the warmth slip away with the material. Her skin was instantly covered with goose-bumps. She reached over to the small chair that sat beneath the window. It was an old chair that had been passed down through her grandfather's family. The wood was heavy and hand carved; the upholstery cream colored with a hand embroidered floral pattern on it. Lately it had been the spot where she hung her sports bra and running pants. She chastised herself and made a mental note to try and stop using the antique chair as a clothes hamper. She pulled the sports bra on over her head and stood up to put on her running pants. They made a "swishing" sound like two plastic bags rubbing up against each other as she put her feet into them. They were cold on her skin and she shivered a little.

She was disappointed that soon she would have to start turning on the heat at night. She walked over to her dresser drawers, pulled out a pair of white cotton ankle socks, and sat back on the bed to put them on. Once she was content with the way the seam felt on the tops of her toes, she leaned over and grabbed her shoes; her good old trusty Nike running sneakers. Alex started putting them on, all the while thinking of how Abuela would also not have approved of the fact that she hadn't been for a run since she died. She just couldn't muster the energy or desire to push herself out the door. Hiding away in her home, mostly curled up in bed under the safety of her covers, for the last few days had seemed like the only option for her since the funeral. She smiled a little as she slipped her sneakers on. They were cold, and they felt good as she guided her feet inside them. She brushed her long hair and pulled it back into a ponytail. An old, ratty, long-sleeved t-shirt stamped

"Holy Cross" would be her running partner today, and she pulled it on. She walked into the bathroom and brushed her teeth, enjoying the tingling feel of the toothpaste. She let her tongue slip over her slick, clean teeth once she was done. A quick face wash and halfhearted towel dry followed. Alex walked over to the bedroom window, unlatched the lock, and pushed it open. The cool breeze that met her face was crisp and smelled clean. She inhaled it through her nostrils, deep into her lungs, savoring its freshness. She smiled a real smile for the first time since her grandmother died.

CHAPTER THREE

HE WOKE TO THE SOUND OF THE TRAIN RUMBLING BY AS it shook the walls, threatening to knock down the only picture he had of his mother. He groaned and grabbed his head. It pounded loudly, the pulse of his temples threatening to explode through his skin. The room began to spin, and he cursed himself for drinking the entire bottle of whiskey last night. He had been thinking of her as he drank the burning liquid and managed to pleasure himself twice before passing out half naked. He winced as he rolled over on the bed.

The sunlight invaded the darkness through the small window, the only window in his basement studio apartment. It was cold and moldy, but it was cheap and had come without any questions. Dust flew up in a cloud around him, little speckles of it visible in the sunlight. He sneezed three times, again cursing the empty whiskey bottle on the floor and the allergies he had acquired as a kid. The digital clock on the nightstand read six thirty a.m. *Alex should be drinking her coffee right now. She must be sad still*, he thought. He felt a pang of sympathy for her. He knew she had only had her grandmother all these years. Since that first day he saw her, he had been researching her at the local library, pulling out any information he could find on her. They had all the old newspaper articles on microfiche film, and he learned how to use the old technology quickly. He read the news-clipping from when she was nine and her parents died in a car accident. It said that it had been a very snowy evening and the car skidded off the road into a ravine. He remembered the picture of her parents, thinking that Alex had looked a lot like her father but had probably gotten her eyes from her mother. It was hard to tell, though, because everything was in black and white. *I would have liked to have met her mother back in the day*, he thought. She had been a very beautiful woman. *I would have shown her a really good time.* He smiled slightly as he mindlessly touched the scar that ran vertically down almost the full length of his chest, its pink slightly tough tissue unmoving under the light pressure of his fingertips.

He wondered briefly how Alex would have been as a psychologist for him. He had been to many psychologists since his mother died and they hauled his asshole father off to jail. In and out of foster homes, the case workers made him attend regular psychiatric evaluations. *What a fucking joke*, he thought. He had run away from most of them. Nothing could have ever replaced his mother. His thoughts turned to his mother - his sad, dead mother. *No, she didn't die*, he thought, *she was murdered.* Anger flashed across his face as the blood rushed into his head, turing his already pounding headache into a thundering torrent of pain. He grabbed the sides of his head, pulling on the thick blonde hair that had been matted down to his head with sweat during sleep. *Stop it*, the voice inside said. *Don't think about it. She died. That is all.*

"No! She was murdered. I saw the blood." he spoke out loud.

Don't think about it. Take some slow, deep breaths. It wasn't your fault.

"It was my fault. I watched her die and did nothing. She drowned in her own blood, choking, gulping for air." He whispered to the empty room.

Tears streamed down his large face now. *There was nothing you could do. You were just a little kid.* The voice inside was that of his last shrink, the one that tried to teach him how to control "the evil." He used a few of the coping mechanisms the shrink had taught him sometimes when he needed to calm down. "The evil" had been born the same day his mother died. It taunted him, teased him, coaxed him. It raced through his head on an almost constant basis. The black hole that tried to suck him in since his mother's death - "the evil"- made him do some really bad things in his lifetime. He had been so grateful to his last shrink for showing him a way to try and stifle it. It was too bad his last shrink had to go away.

It wasn't too bad, he deserved it. A new voice emerged, now the evil spoke.

"Yes, it was too bad," he argued. It was awful that he had to silence him once he found out the truth about him, about what he had done.

He would have tattled on you, you idiot. You had to get rid of him. The evil yelled.

"He was my friend," he said as he shrank into the pillow.

He was no friend. He only pretended to be a friend. You are a fucking loser! Why would anyone want to be your friend? No one wants to be your friend. You are alone now, and you always will be. The evil taunted him, screamed at him. He squeezed his eyes shut trying to will it away.

"Shut up, shut up, you don't know" he yelled, eyes shut.

I do know. Your own father hated you. Wished you had never been born. Why would anyone want to be your friend????

"Please, shut up," he begged. His voice echoed in the sparsely furnished room. Sweat poured from him, the smell a combination of cigarettes, whiskey, and sex.

He had to do something. He had to silence the beast, the evil within him. He took a deep breath and counted to ten, letting the air out slowly. His shrink had taught him that. He did this ten times. When he had finished the evil had gone, the pounding had gone, and the storm had gone. He sighed in relief and laid his head back down on his pillow. Once the surge had passed he grew calm again. After what seemed like hours, he thought about what he would do today. It was a Tuesday morning and he didn't have to be at the cable company until nine.

He worked for Connections Cable Company and had been there for a few months. He liked doing it. It was the longest he had ever held a job. Two or three months was a long time for him. Even though he was only twenty-five years old, he had already had many jobs. He had done everything from pumping gas to cleaning horse stalls at a local horse farm when he had lived down south. *Putting cable into people's homes is much more rewarding*, he thought to himself as a smile formed on his face. He was surprised he had made it this long. His anger helped him lose his other jobs quickly, but he had been really working on keeping it under control lately. As long as they didn't connect him with the two dead housewives he would be fine. He didn't want to get fired from this job. He liked the feeling of being let into people's homes, trusted to roam through their most sacred places. He even felt a little dirty when he saw the beds of people and imagined what they did there. He felt himself getting hard as he thought of different couples making love in the different bedrooms he had seen over the last few months.

He thought of the two housewives. He hadn't been able to help himself. They had asked him into their bedrooms. They asked him for sex. They asked him to kill them. He tried to control himself. He hadn't wanted to kill them, but their eyes begged and their bodies pleaded.

He glanced over at the digital clock once more and read the large numbers, seven fifteen. *What the hell*, he thought, *I have time*. He began to touch himself, and his thoughts shifted back to Alex and what he would do to her when he finally had the chance. He ejaculated at the final image he had of being on top of her, his hands around her throat.

CHAPTER FOUR

ALEX RAN UP TO THE STEPS OF HER HOME, OUT OF BREATH
and a little disappointed in herself. *It is amazing how in a week or so
of not running I am already out of shape, she thought.* She opened the
door and caught herself. Her heart dropped like a boulder into the pit
of her stomach. Years of repetition, day after day going on runs, day
after day of walking into the house, day after day of knowing when she
walked in the house … she gasped, overwhelmed with grief. She had
been waiting to smell the boiling beans, tortillas hot off the stove, and
fresh bread baking in the oven. Yet no smells floated to her. Nothing
came to her except for the stifling realization that there was no fresh
bread in the oven because there was no Abuela to make it. She took in a
deep breath and squeezed her eyes shut, momentarily willing the tears
away. She swallowed hard and stood up tall, as tall as she could make
herself. Her heart pounded in her chest, not from the run, but from the
guilt; the guilt of allowing herself to forget for even a second that her
grandmother was no longer with her.

She walked into the house, closing the front door behind her.
She entered the living room without taking off her shoes and fell onto

the couch with a thud, not caring that her sweat seeped into the smooth beige cushions. *Stop it, Alex,* she chastised. *Abuela would be so mad at you right now..* Her muscles ached, her head pounded, and her chin quivered. *I will not cry*, she thought, just as the tears began to slip down her cheeks mixing with the perspiration that had begun to dry there. *I will not cry. This is it. No more.* She stood on slightly shaky legs and willed herself to the shower. *I am done mourning. Now I just need to remember. Abuela would want that.*

Alex got undressed and threw her sweaty clothes into the dirty clothes hamper. She turned on the shower and looked at herself in the mirror. Her face was drawn. Large, dark half moon circles seemed to have taken permanent residence under her eyes. Steam from the hot water began to cover the mirror, distorting her image as if she were magically disappearing under the guise of a smoke screen. She slid her hand across it, leaving behind a streak of water spots, then stepped into the shower. The water was almost too hot for her, but she didn't care. She was trying to wash away the pain, scrub away the sadness. The steam continued to fill the small bathroom, the fan working hard to remove it. Shower water pelted her skin, her breasts, and her face like little hot bullets, leaving red marks all over her body. She took it, not turning away, needing to feel something, to feel anything but the sorrow. She thought of her life, of the people in her life that she loved, how they all were taken away, stolen from her. Why? What had she done that was so bad? Why was she cursed? Abuela never understood why she didn't want to find love, didn't try to foster friendships. Couldn't she see? She couldn't stand any more pain, any more emptiness, any more hardship. A cool breeze floated in from the bathroom window, fighting against the heat of the shower. As the water fell so did her tears. *This will be the last time I cry,* she promised herself again, *The very last time.*

She dried off while she considered what she could do to make herself feel better. She decided she needed to get out of the house. She would go into the office. Even though she had no patients scheduled for today, she needed to feel the comfort of being somewhere other than here. She used the towel to pull the extra water from her hair and walked into her bedroom.

She wished she hadn't opened her window before showering because the frigid air that hit her was a stark contrast to the heat of the steamy, warm bathroom. It almost froze her on the spot. She winced a little at the cold, then continued to get ready. She put on a little make-up, mainly to cover her raccoon eyes, and brushed her long wet hair. Normally she dried it, but today she pulled it up into a tight bun. She dressed in a gray skirt with matching blazer, a white silk tank underneath. Her black high heels seemed like too much work for today, so she opted for the black flats she bought a few months ago. She didn't need pantyhose. Her smooth olive-skinned legs were beautiful naked. She glanced at herself in the mirror, not so much for approval, but more so to make sure she was decent enough to be seen. When she was satisfied, she turned and left the house.

The car smelled musty. She hadn't driven it since the funeral. She started the engine and rolled down all the windows. It was still chilly outside, but she could use the fresh air and so could the car. The radio hummed quietly, some James Taylor song she had heard many times before. As she pulled out of the driveway, she had to slam on the brakes.

"Oh my god", she gasped.

Tommy Johnson came flying out from behind her car on his bicycle, waving and smiling. *I almost hit him, for God's sake*, she thought. He was oblivious to what had almost happened, and she was left with a heart that was about to explode out of her chest. *Kids*, she thought shaking her head. Then smiled as she remembered the time she had almost given Abuela a heart attack.

It was a sunny day, warm enough for her to ride her bike. She had just the week before learned how to ride without training wheels. Abuela had been watching her from the front yard. Up and down the street, up and down the street. Alex had been feeling more and more confident with each passing ride. She decided to take off from the slight hill of the driveway instead of the sidewalk where she had been the entire time. What she hadn't become very good at yet were the brakes. As she flew down the driveway into the street, a car had come barreling down the street at the same time. The driver slammed on his brakes, and Alex slammed head on into a parked car across the street. She hadn't even tried to apply her brakes. Abuela screamed from the driveway, running quickly for an old woman. She spoke a combination of English and Spanish, mostly swears. Alex was old enough to know the swears in Spanish by then, and if she hadn't been so stunned she would have had to bite her tongue to keep from laughing. She remembered Abuela ripping her up from the ground - angry at first, scared to death, and then, just relieved that Alex was okay. That was short lived because once Abuela knew Alex had no life threatening wounds she had grounded her from her bike for a week. Then, to top it all off, the driver of the car that had been moving just a little too fast had yelled a few choice words for her before driving off.

Alex smiled again at the memory. This time no tears came. Her chin quivered a bit but she continued to smile. Alex backed up the rest of the way and drove down to the end of her street. She paused for a moment wondering if she were doing the right thing going into work so soon, then decided, *yes*, she needed this.

CHAPTER FIVE

ALEX OPENED THE FRONT DOOR TO HER OFFICE AND crept in like she was stealing something. She knew Manny and her assistant Lola wouldn't be happy with her that she hadn't taken more time off. She smiled a little. They were always just a little over-protective. The dark paneling in the waiting area welcomed her. The empty chairs sat along the wall, beckoning for someone, anyone, to fill them with warmth. Fluorescent lights buzzed above and made her squint a little. She walked through the main waiting area back towards her office and, as she got close to her door, pulled out the key. She paused a moment to look at the smoky glass window that boasted her name, **Dr. Alex Aguilar --** her Mexican heritage, her father's last name, Abuela's last name. *I am the last of the Aguilar line*, she thought. She took a deep breath and opened the door.

Alex looked at her desk. The dark cherry wood had been hand-carved by a local furniture maker; "a one of a kind piece," he told her. The dim lamp on her desk cast a warm glow in her otherwise dark office. A brighter lamp sat behind her desk but she opted not to turn it on just yet. She sank into the chair behind the desk, so large that it seemed to almost swallow her whole. It was one of those fancy high-backed leather chairs that people pay a lot of money for in order to look important. She grimaced. She had let a well known interior decorator take care of making the office look professional. She was never very good at those kinds of things. She was here for her patients, not to look important. The interior decorator had insisted that leather and dark wood was the way to go. Alex didn't argue, just wrote the check and handed it over. She ran her hand over the smooth wood and let it stop just short of the stack of papers and patient files. The smell from the leather patient couch and the other large, overstuffed leather chair where she would sit sometimes to take notes filled her nostrils with a familiar thickness. She got up and moved from the chair behind the desk to the comfy chair. She sat for a moment rubbing her hands lightly on the puffy arms, soft under her palms. The leather was smooth to the touch, warm yet cool. The velvety texture felt good under her fingertips. She laid her head back against the chair and closed her eyes.

The smell of freshly brewed coffee floated to her on an imaginary breeze. She raised her head from the chair, feeling a little foggy. *How long have I been sitting here*? Had she actually fallen asleep? Just then, Manny poked his head into her office.

"Hey." He beamed a glorious smile at her.

"Hey, yourself," she smiled back, not surprised to see him there. She was actually a bit relieved. "I see your spare key to my office has come in handy again," she said.

"Hey!" he cried, feigning hurt. "I tried calling your house and when you didn't answer I had the worst feeling that you were here with your nose stuck inside some kind of patient file, begging me telepathically to come save you." He gave her a disapproving look that told her he thought it was too soon for her to be back at work. She knew it would come, she was waiting for it.

She looks tired, he thought. Her eyes didn't have the twinkle they usually held and dark circles betrayed her lack of sleep. He noticed she tried to cover them with make-up. She didn't always wear it, nor did she need to. Her face was beautiful, her complexion flawless. He allowed his eyes to linger on her for a moment longer before turning away. He didn't want to stare too long. He had tried so hard to make her believe that he only thought of her as a friend and colleague since she had thwarted his attempts at something more so long ago.

"I brought you a fresh cup of java," he laughed. Alex smiled her gratitude. *He knows me so well,* she thought. It was nice to be here with him right now, exactly what she needed, a friend. He smiled warmly back at her. She knew he was worried about her. She needed to somehow reassure him that she was alright.

"You can't expect me to stay home and let all these patients of mine run around unsupervised, can you?" she asked with a light laugh.

He loved her laugh. This was her "cute" laugh, almost forced from what he could tell. What he really loved to hear was her belly laugh. He first heard it in college. They had an ice storm the night before they had planned to meet at the library to study. He had just gotten an A on a paper he had written, or rather, agonized over. She was at the bottom of the hill waiting for him. When he saw her, he had gotten so excited to tell her about the grade that he started to run, forgetting about the ice on the ground. As he began to slide down the hill she looked worried at first as his feet flailed out from underneath him. Barely catching his footing, he slid off the pathway, his feet like ice skates. He flew face first into a pile of snow that had been strategically placed there just for him it seemed. She burst out laughing. She laughed so hard and so true, a deep belly laugh. She laughed until tears ran down her cheeks, on the verge of hiccups. At first he was so embarrassed that he got upset with her for laughing at him. But her laugh had been so real, so beautiful, that his embarrassment dissipated. Now looking at her in the dim light of the office with her sad eyes and black circles, he longed to hear her laugh.

He handed her the coffee, steam spilling over the brim of the cup, careful not to spill the hot liquid. He noticed as she took it that her hand seemed a bit shaky. He tried to ignore it. He unconsciously pushed a piece of hair off of her forehead and looked deep into her eyes, searching. She knew he wanted to talk, really talk, but she wasn't sure she was ready for it yet.

"I know what that look is, Manny, and I don't think I am ready just yet." She sighed.

He looked caught off guard, confused and worried at the same time. Alex felt guilty. She wanted to talk to him; really. She just didn't know what she wanted to say. Her lips came together as if she were going to say something, but decided against it and looked away. She stared at her desk for a moment.

"Wow, looks like I have a lot of work to catch up on, so....." she paused, looking at him. Manny looked from her, to her desk, and back to her and nodded. *He understood, didn't he?* she wondered. He stood up, came over to her, bent down and kissed her forehead. She smiled at him, again in thanks, and patted the strong hand he had placed on her shoulder.

"I have the day off. I was wondering if we might grab some lunch or even dinner? We need to go over the Grafton Hill Strangler case now that you're back. We have some new leads that came in and a few possibilities in the witness department." he said.

"Um, okay. I think I could use a little dinner. Your treat right?" she joked.

She knew the answer. It was always Manny's treat. No matter how hard she had protested in the last ten years, she had not once been able to pay the check for any meal they ever shared together. Now she said it to him just to tease him. It never phased him and never got her any closer to being able to pay the bill.

"Claro que si, of course!" he said.

Just then Alex heard the ceremonious creak of the front door to the office. A familiar voice rang out, slightly off key, filling the office.

"Hola," she sang as she poked her head into Alex's office, mimicking the same entrance as Manny - except that Manny hadn't sung to her. Every morning it was the same thing, a singing hello from a short, slightly chubby, fifty-something woman named Lola Martinez; her high heels clapping to the silent beat she always seemed to keep in her head. Today she wore a lime green pants suit that fit just a little too snug and canary yellow high heels with matching canary yellow headband, earrings, and bracelets. Her hair was dyed black to cover the gray hair she had started sprouting a few years back. Today she had it pulled up in a high ponytail with a large mountain of bangs puffed up at the crest of her forehead. Her thick black eyeliner rimmed large brown eyes, and bright red blush that didn't quite fit her dark complexion sat on chubby cheeks. Her eye shadow was a pale green color. Alex imagined she must have had a hard time finding lime green in the make-up section. Lola looked like she belonged in South Beach, Florida. It was hard to believe she lived here in Massachusetts. She had a deep voice for a woman, raspy from the Winston cigarettes she smoked and lined with a thick Latina accent. She was originally from Ponce, Puerto Rico, but had moved here with her family when she was nineteen.

"Hey, Lola," Alex sang back, smiling.

"What are ju doing here, Miss Alex?" Lola asked, sounding a little surprised.

"Nice to see you too, Lola." Alex laughed.

"No, no, Miss Alex. That is not what I meant," Lola stumbled, obviously thinking Alex was upset with her. "Hi, Mr. Manny. How are ju doing?" she asked, trying to change the tone.

"Hola, Lola." Manny smiled at the sound of the two words put together every time he said it, knowing how funny and poetic it sounded. They all usually laughed together when he said it, but today no one laughed. He could sense how uncomfortable Lola had made herself. So could Alex.

"Oh Lola, I knew what you meant. I am happy to be here. I needed to get back to my work, you know? Esta bien, no te preocupes. It's fine, don't worry." Alex smiled at Lola, who looked like a child being scolded for eating cookies before dinnertime.

"Oh jes, Miss Alex," Lola said. "When my Carlos died I had to get right back to work so I wouldn't sit around being sad, ju know?" No sooner than the words had come out, Lola raised her hand to her mouth as if she was trying to catch them and shove them back in. Her eyes widened in surprise at herself. Again she had made herself uncomfortable. She shifted her plump feet back and forth on the floor. Alex knew as soon as she saw Lola's eyes and the expression on her face that she felt like she had stuck her foot in her mouth again. She knew Lola hadn't meant anything bad by what she had said, but before Alex could say anything Lola was apologizing….

"Oh, Dios Mio, I am so sorry, Miss Alex, I didn't mean….."

Alex held up her hand to cut her off before she could say anymore, or feel any worse. "Lola, it is fine. It was fine what you said, and I accept your apology even though you have nothing to apologize for."

"Okay, Miss Alex, I'll go to work now." Lola gave one last apologetic smile to Alex, and turned to go to her desk. The sound of her low voice singing and the rhythmic click clack of her heels as she walked away was comforting to Alex. *Nice to be back to work,* she thought.

"Well, I guess I will call you in a little while." Manny smiled and gently touched her face. Her skin was soft and warm under his fingertips.

"Yeah, okay. I will talk to you later. I have to get through a bit of work here before I can go anywhere." She smiled, a little overwhelmed it seemed. Manny turned to leave but not before he flashed her one more brilliant smile.

"See ya later, Alligator." he quipped.

"Okie dokie, Smokey," she smiled back.

Alex watched him as he left and felt blessed to have such a great friend. She sighed slightly, content for the moment. She felt good being here. She felt useful again, happy to be back at work. She walked over to her desk and looked at the stacks of files piled neatly on top of the desk. *Oh man, maybe not super happy to be back to work after all*, she thought, shaking her head slightly as a small half smile appeared on her lips.

CHAPTER SIX

HE SAT OUTSIDE THE LARGE COLONIAL HOME FRAMED BY its manicured lawn and two-car garage. Birds chirped background songs in the trees for the squirrels as they scurried back and forth from tree branch to tree branch gathering nuts for the winter. The leaves had already started to change colors; deep reds, browns, and yellows blanketing the lawns and streets. He watched for a few more minutes then turned and rolled up the van window.

He picked up his clipboard to check and make sure this was the right house. *Yep*, he thought, *234 Putnum Road.* Lugging his large frame out of the company van, he lumbered up the stone walkway toward the heavy oak door with its silver knocker. He used the doorbell, ringing it twice, his large leather gloved finger completely covering the small button as he pushed. The muffled sound of the chiming bell summoned its home's occupant. He waited patiently, surveying the layout of the lawn, the garage, the windows, and the neighborhood. The deep hum of a lawnmower could be heard a few houses down, drowning out the lesser of the neighborhood garble. Just then the door swung open and a dark haired woman in her late thirties stood before him.

"Well, hello there." The woman at the door smiled, bright red lipstick smudged onto her two front teeth. *Looks like blood*, he thought, as he smiled back at her.

He is handsome, she mused to herself. His blonde hair was just short of wild. It crowned a wide jaw line, a nose that had been broken more than a few times, and dark pools of black for eyes. But when he smiled, something fluttered in her stomach. *Too much bourbon,* she thought.

"Hello yourself, Mrs....?" He asked as he looked down at his clipboard searching for her name on the order form.

"Mzzz. Bowen" she corrected.

He got that sometimes in this line of work. Divorced or married it didn't matter. All that mattered was that most were lonely house-wives looking to have a little twist thrown into their otherwise boring daily routine.

"Okay, Mzzz. Bowen," he said, letting her know he heard her loudly and clearly. "Where do you need to be plugged in?" He laughed inside his head at what he had just said, noticing how sexual it sounded. She must have thought the same thing because a sly smile came across her face. She motioned him into the house.

The entryway was beautiful - tiled floor, a small crystal chan-delier hanging just above his head, and a mahogany table on which you could throw your keys, your mail, or whatever, but wouldn't because it was too expensive. She turned her back to him and started to walk towards the living room. She had on tight black stretch pants with dainty little black heels, the kind with the cheesy black feathers and bow on the front, that clicked as she walked. She had a slightly sexy swagger and a tight rear. He thought she smelled delicious, floral perfume mixed with the scent of liquor. *What was it? Ah, bourbon,* he thought. She walked into the large living room and he followed, his feet sinking into the bog of beige plush carpet that lay wall to wall. There was a large white leather sectional sofa with many overstuffed pillows strategically placed here and there. Cathedral ceilings and massive windows let in brilliant sunlight. She smiled as she turned to face him and pointed to the television. It was a 62-inch wide screen, high definition television. He looked around the expansive room and was amazed at what money could buy.

"This one first, please." She smiled again, this time a little more slyly.

He could sense something about her. Something seeped from her, what was it? He had felt that kind of thing before; sexual tension, desire, a need to be needed.

"My *ex*-husband just paid for that bad boy," she smiled. She again put emphasis on the word *ex*. It hissed from her mouth like a snake taunting its prey.

He took his tool belt and one of the two cable boxes he had brought with him and began to work. As he bent over the entertainment stand she watched him. He could feel her eyes all over him. The muscles in his arms rippled with just the slightest movements. His backside was taut in his extra tight jeans. A drip of sweat fell from his forehead to his arm, and she watched as it crawled down his bicep and hit the floor. It appeared to happen in slow motion. She licked her lips unconsciously.

"The other set is upstairs in *my room,*" she almost whispered the last part. "I will be up there waiting for you to plug me in," she said. He smiled, his back still to her. She turned and went up the stairs. He thought about it while he finished hooking up the cable box. *She certainly is attractive enough*, he thought. It wouldn't be the first time he had done this. *This was one of the perks of the job, right?*

He walked up the wooden stairs, half expecting them to creak. But the newly varnished wood beneath his boots told a different story. *Which room is hers?* he wondered as he climbed the stairs. Soon he didn't have to wonder anymore. From the last door at the end of the hall soft music floated to him, calling him. He opened the bedroom door and saw her there on the bed. She had changed into a black negligee but had left her black heels on. He smiled. Her black hair lay all around her on the king-sized pillow. The blood red silk pillow case almost matched her lipstick.

"Hey there," she smiled.

He looked her up and down, appraising her like one would a piece of meat. He watched, with anticipation, as she moved her hand between her thighs. When she spread her legs, crotchless panties exposed the smooth folds of skin and a finely manicured finger moving back and forth. He swallowed as he felt himself get excited. He moved over to the bed and stood next to her. With her free hand she began to massage the bulge that had begun to grow inside his well-fitting jeans. He moved her hand away from the inside of her thighs and replaced it with his own. He imagined her skin would be warm and wet with eagerness. He moved his gloved finger around lightly at first, then with a little more pressure. *Wish I could feel her, without this damned glove,* he thought. The thought quickly fled as her hands moved to unbutton his pants. He helped her pull them down and gasped as she took him into her mouth.

"Oh God," he moaned.

Her mouth was warm and wet. She couldn't take him even halfway in. He was much too big for her when he was fully erect. Her tongue danced around his tip, tickling, teasing. She giggled, and he smiled. *She is good,* he thought. He leaned over to lick one of her nipples then bit down gently. She moaned as he brought her to the brink.

"Please," she whispered. "I want you inside me".

He was just waiting for her to say the words. He climbed on top of her. She was so small under him, and she cried out as he entered her. Again, he was too big. She couldn't take him all in. It didn't matter. He felt so good, and she moaned again and again.

"Oh god, you feel so good," she cried.

He put his full weight on her and moved faster than before. This time she cried in ecstasy and pain. He began to sweat from the exertion. Faster and faster he moved; louder and louder she cried. He moved his hands all over her breasts, her hips, her thighs, back up to her breasts, and then up to her throat. She moaned again as he caressed her throat. He put his hands around her neck, gently at first. She smiled at this, as if she liked it.

He kept thrusting, harder and faster, until he was ripping her. She cried out in surprise, not pleasure. Her hands flew up and gripped at his arms, digging her nails into the biceps she had admired not so long ago. All she felt was pain. She screamed, and he planted a gloved hand firmly over her mouth. Faster and faster, god, he couldn't go any faster. He was climaxing and squeezing her throat tighter and tighter. He could feel her legs kicking beneath him, but he barely noticed. Her arms were flailing about, and she may have hit him once or twice, nothing hard enough to pull him from his pleasured state.

He ejaculated inside her just as he squeezed the last bit of life out of her. His head was spinning. He climbed off of Mzzz. Bowen and knelt next to her on the bed, staring off into another world in deep thought. He suddenly heard panting from somewhere in the room. He looked around, angry that someone had come home, when he realized it was coming from him. He chuckled softly at his paranoia. Once his heart stopped racing, he looked down at his latest victim.

Her eyes bulged out of her head, capillaries broken inside, blood lining the whites of her eyeballs, little road maps to nowhere. He sat there for a while longer, caressing her lifeless body, whispering to her… "Oh, Alex, Alex, sweet, beautiful Alex….."

CHAPTER SEVEN

ALEX PRACTICALLY STUMBLED INTO THE CAFE. SHE WAS drenched with sweat and breathing heavily, yet she still managed an exquisite smile.

"Hey, Amanda. How are you doing today?" she breathed.

Amanda, the young girl behind the counter, smiled back at her. She was the same girl there everyday, and she asked the same question everyday: "the usual Alex?" Her smile was always bright and warm. She wore thick black glasses and her normally mousy brown hair was recently on the receiving end of a very bad bleach job. It was pulled back from her face with several strategically placed bobby pins and a ponytail holder. She appeared very messy to someone who didn't know her, but Alex could tell she had taken great care to look like she didn't care. She had on thick black eyeliner and a little too much blush. She was probably only twenty or twenty-one, but her high-pitched voice made her sound like she was ten. Alex loved her to death. She knew she had been through a lot in her short years on earth. Alex noticed very pale scars on the inside of Amanda's wrists that she generally hid with a watch on one and some bracelets on the other. Alex was trained to notice things like that, but sometimes she wished she didn't. It saddened her to think such a sweet girl as Amanda could have been sad enough or angry enough to want to kill herself.

"Yes please," Alex answered.

She looked around the cafe and smiled at people. There weren't many of them there this morning. Some of the regulars were there, and they smiled back at her. She smiled at the blonde man in the corner. He sat quietly with his coffee and newspaper. It seemed to be the same thing everyday. He always sat in the corner. He always looked at her a little strangely, as if she made him uncomfortable. But he seemed harmless enough. She found it a little funny that such a large man would fit himself into the dainty little cafe chairs pushed up into a corner. It must have taken a lot of work to squeeze past the crowded tables and chairs just to get back into that corner. She also found it funny the thought that *she* would make *him* feel uncomfortable. She had been smiling at him lately, but he seemed to always look quickly away when she did. Maybe he was really shy. She had thought yesterday that maybe she wouldn't smile at him anymore. But she was in such a good mood this morning that she had totally forgotten and beamed a real beauty his way. Again, he seemed nervous or uncomfortable and turned away. *Maybe he doesn't like women*, she thought, as she almost laughed out loud. She had to quickly stifle the giggle that threatened to escape her lips. She pretended to cough instead.

"Here you go, Alex." Amanda flashed her pretty smile as she handed Alex her iced coffee, "a little milk, one sugar."

"Thanks, Amanda," Alex said and handed Amanda a five dollar bill. "Keep the change. And have a great day, too." Alex turned and left the cafe.

The day was chilly. Winter was setting in, and she had worn an overly large sweatshirt for her run this morning. It had been three months since her grandmother had passed and, for the most part, Alex had gotten back to a somewhat normal life. She walked down the block and made a left. The cafe was only a mile from her house and the walk was always nice. The cold wind blew around her and cooled her sweaty skin. The iced coffee cup was frozen in her hand, and she switched it to the other hand every few minutes to prevent what felt like near frostbite. *I'm going to have to start getting hot coffee soon,* she considered as the sun started to crest. She walked the last few blocks to her house. She gazed around, admiring the well kept lawns and listening to the sounds of people getting ready for work and leaving their homes. Cars started driving down the streets. It was quite a change from when she first started out in the mornings; dark sky, quiet neighborhoods, and no humming cars moving by.

She climbed the few steps of her front porch and stopped short of the front door. A long brown box lay on the front porch with a yellow UPS slip attached to it. She was a little surprised. She never got packages here, not counting the flowers she had received when Abuela passed. She bent over and picked up the box with one hand as she held her iced coffee. The box was relatively light. She was quite curious as to what was inside. She hurried into the house, excited to open it. She went into the kitchen and laid everything down on the old wooden table that her grandfather had made.

She hadn't known him because he had died when she was a baby, but she had heard wonderful stories about him. He had been a Mexican immigrant, crossing the border into Texas when he was 18 years old and working to get his citizenship from day one. He had worked in cotton fields and oil fields, eventually ending up as an apprentice for a carpenter who taught him everything he knew. Abuela told her what a great man her grandfather had been. When Abuela and her grandfather had her mother they were still young. Abuela said Alex's grandfather had a big opportunity to join the Carpenter's Union on the East Coast so they had moved here, bought land, and built the house. Her own parents had lived here also when she was first born. They had been very young and were struggling to get on their feet. She smiled at the memories she had learned from Abuela. She had a great history, one she was very proud of.

She grabbed a pair of scissors from the kitchen drawer and cut at the twine that held the box together. She opened up the lid and gasped. Inside were black roses. The petals were wilting and the smell was putrid. Her heart began to race. *Why would someone send dead flowers? Black, dead flowers?* Her hand trembled as she reached for the small white envelope inside. She wasn't sure who would do something like this.

Maybe they weren't meant for me, she thought. Before she had her fingers wrapped around the envelope, she changed her mind and searched for the delivery slip instead. There it was - her name, Alexandra Aguilar, with the correct address and all. She dropped the slip on the table and again reached for the small white envelope. She picked it up and slowly opened it. As she did the edge of the paper sliced the tip of her finger. She winced at the pain.

"Damn it!" she cursed. A small drop of blood fell onto the envelope, smearing slightly. She stuck her finger tip in her mouth and sucked on it for a second, her mind racing with confusion and trepidation. Inside the envelope was a thin piece of paper. She opened it to see small black letters written messily. The paper had no lines and the writing appeared as if it had been done by a child. She read it and read it again:

Hello Alex,

I have been watching you. Only a beautiful flower such as you deserves

beautiful flowers such as these.
All my love,
Your secret admirer

Her heart sank and her breath became shallow. Who had been watching her? She looked around her house frantically for a sign, anything that would help her figure this out. What exactly was she looking for? She didn't have the slightest idea what to do. Her first thought was Manny. She ran over to the phone that hung on the kitchen wall, picked it up, and dialed his number. He answered on the third ring.

"Detective Castillo here."

"Manny! Thank God! I didn't know what to do, so I called you."

Manny could hear Alex's excitement through the phone.

"Alex, what is wrong? What is going on? Are you okay? Where are you?" Manny threw the questions at her faster than she could process them. She had to calm down. She had to catch her breath. She took two deep breaths and then answered.

"I just got a box delivered to my house, on my front porch, Manny." There was a pause on the other side.

"Okay, so what is wrong?"

"The box, Manny. It had dead, black roses in it."

"Wow. OK. That's not what I was expecting to hear," Manny said, clearly confused.

"I know," Alex agreed. "And that wasn't the worst part. There was a note."

"What did it say?" Manny sounded more urgent and worried now.

"It said, 'I have been watching you.'" Alex's voice cracked.

CHAPTER EIGHT

HE KNEW HE WAS TAKING A CHANCE BEING HERE IN THE daytime, but he had to see her face when she got the flowers. He had practically run out of the cafe after she left, almost tripping over an elderly woman. She had yelled at him, "Watch it, buddy!" Normally that would have made him laugh, but not today. He had to get there before she did. He drove the opposite way on different side streets than what she would walk. He didn't want her to see him. She knew him from the cafe now. She had even been looking at him and smiling at him lately. He shivered with delight as he thought of this. She seemed a little happier lately. It had been about three months since her grandmother had died and she appeared to be getting over it.

He had once again parked a few houses down from hers, but his time he chose to park four houses down instead of two. The sun was shining brightly now, and she would easily spot him from two houses away. He wasn't worried. His new pair of binoculars would allow him to see her face when she found the package he had left for her on the front porch.

As he sat waiting, he thought about the cafe. Right before she walked in he had seen the report in the Daily News on the second page:

Ex-wife of Prominent Lawyer Found Slain

> *Ex-wife of John Bowen, a prominent lawyer and partner of Lockney-Bowen Law Firm of the Metro-west area, was found yesterday in her home by her house-keeper. It appears that Mrs. Bowen had been raped and strangled in her own bed. Detective Manuel Castillo of the Newbury Police Department and lead detective in the investigation, stated that they have some leads but are unable to give further information at this time.....*

He read the first few lines again and again. *Damn that Detective Castillo.* Just the name made him angry. He had seen Manny Castillo with Alex many times since he started watching her. He didn't think they were lovers. He had never seen Manny sleeping over, leaving quietly in the morning. He did know they were close, though. He hated Manny. He hated that Manny got to be so close to her. *I should be the one close to her, smelling her, touching her. What gave him the right? What made him so special?* He read that the two went to college together and over the past few years had successfully partnered up to solve quite a few murder cases in the Metro-West area. Still, what did she see in him? He was so much better than Manny. His body was tighter, bigger, stronger. He was much smarter. Someday when he had his chance he would show her, prove to her that he was the better man.

When the anger passed, his mind switched to the newspaper article and the fear set in. *What if they knew it was him?* So far the police said they didn't have any suspects, but that didn't mean that they wouldn't find out that someone had been there to install the cable. Once they figured that out, they would want to talk to him. He hadn't been back to work since he had left her there, naked and cold. He had cleaned the work van up, trying to remove any fingerprints he might have left behind, and had parked it in the same place he had taken it from. He didn't think anyone besides Stella had actually seen him that morning. She was the one who handed out the paperwork to all the techs, gave them all their routes, and checked them in and out. He would have to take care of her before the cops got around to speaking with her. There was the other problem, too - the little problem that he had left inside *Ms. Bowen*. He hadn't meant to go all the way. He wasn't going to let it get that far. Damn, how could he have been so stupid? *Well*, he thought, *at least when I got the job at the cable company I didn't use my real name or address.* He smiled again. This hadn't been his first murder, and it certainly wouldn't be his last.

He was reliving the experience of yesterday, replaying the scenes in his mind, when he saw Alex walking up the block. His heart began to hammer in his chest and the sweat came again. He slumped down in his seat as far as he could, peering over the steering wheel just enough to see her. He reached over carefully, grabbing at the seat next to him until he felt his hand touch the cold metal of the binoculars. He pulled them to his face, placing them quickly to his eyes.

The image was blurry at first. It took a couple of seconds for him to adjust his eyes, but he blinked twice and squinted. Then everything became clear and up close. He watched as she climbed the steps and paused when she saw the box. Her face was was full of wonder and curiosity. That made his belly flip. It took her a minute to pick it up before she disappeared into the house. He wished he could see inside the house - see her face when she opened the box, hear her laugh, and see how happy she would be when she got the flowers. He had purchased them two weeks ago. The girl at the flower shop looked at him funny when he had asked for black roses. He said they were for a funeral. She shrugged at him as if she could give two shits. He left them in the box without water so that they would smell beautiful for her when she received them. He enjoyed the smell of rotting flowers and thought she might appreciate it as well.

He sat for another twenty minutes, wondering what the hell she was doing. He could get out and just go take a peak. *No*, he thought, *it is daylight and I can't risk being seen.* He wanted to be able to have a lot of alone time with her once he was able, and he was sure someone would call the police if they saw him creeping around her windows.

Just as he was about to leave, a red Ford Mustang came barreling down the street. The tires screeched to a halt in her driveway. Motherfucker! He knew that car. It belonged to none other than Detective Manny Castillo. *What the fuck is he doing here?* The anger raged inside him.

You could do it now. The evil whispered to him. *You could take him out and do whatever you want to her, right here, right now.*

"No, " he growled, lowly. " I am not going to do it. Not right now, I am not ready."

Of course you are ready. You have been planning this for almost a year now. You can taste it, can't you? His eyes full of surprise as you shoot him down, her screams filling your ears. First she will scream in fear, but then she will scream in pleasure. You know it. Just go. Just be a man, you asshole.

"Stop it." he whispered.

He wanted to scream at the evil but didn't want anyone to hear him. He had to go. *I have to get out of here*, he thought. If he didn't he wasn't sure he could contain the evil. Once Manny had gone into the house, he knew he was safe to leave. He put the keys in the ignition with a very shaky hand, missing the first time he tried. The engine revved and he drove away as fast as he could without bringing any attention to himself. His anger blurred his vision as he drove. His mind raced. He would have to make his move soon or else he was going to explode. He began to laugh as he drove; a deep, guttural laugh that only a madman could produce. *Soon*, he thought, *very soon*.

CHAPTER NINE

THE ROOM SMELLED LIKE ROTTING FLESH MIXED WITH feces and urine. No matter how many times he had done this, it still didn't get any better. The body had been there for quite a long time. The large bedroom almost closed in on him then, small and oppressive, full of stale air and the stench of death. He guessed Mr. Bowen tried to talk to his ex-wife as little as possible as he hadn't called in a missing person's report. The housekeeper, who came every two weeks, was the one who called. According to the Medical Examiner, Ms. Bowen had been dead just about that long. Once they actually got a hold of Mr. Bowen, he finally mentioned that he thought something might have been wrong because Ms. Bowen had missed her monthly supervised visit with the children. Mr. Bowen reported that they figured she was just on one of her drunken benders again. That was the main reason he had finally taken the children and left her, he told them. He gave her the house and a large sum of money just to keep her away from him and the kids. Little did he know it would be much worse than a week of binge drinking that finally killed her. Manny remembered jotting down

Mr. Bowen's name with a question mark on his notepad as a possible suspect but didn't think the spineless weasel had it in him.

She lay on the bed, sprawled out half-naked. She was partially covered by a torn black negligee Manny figured hadn't covered much in the first place. Her face was swollen, with lifeless protruding eyes that accused Manny when he looked at her. Her body was also bloated, her intestines distended and pushing out on her greenish colored skin. The satin sheets beneath her were soiled with dried feces and urine. *God, I hate that smell.*

"Hey, Castillo," the Medical Examiner, Dr. Leavy, interrupted Manny's thoughts.

"Hey Dr. Leavy. She's been here a bit, huh?" Manny asked, knowing the answer.

"Yeah, awhile is right. From the lividity we can tell she most likely died in this position and wasn't moved. The blood stagnated in the back and buttocks. I'm pretty confident when I perform the autopsy I will find that to be the case with the internal organs as well. The blood will have settled along the posterior areas of the lungs, liver, spleen...well, you know..." Leavy trailed off, caught up in her own internal dialogue.

"Well, thankfully it was pretty cool in here so the decomp didn't go as fast as it could have," Manny offered.

"Yes, yes. Well, I will be sure to let you know of alternate findings should there be any as soon as I know. Sure looks like our unsub though, same M.O. We need to get this guy soon, Manny," Dr. Leavy said with a sigh before turning to head back to the CSI team.

The Crime Scene Investigations Unit had already been there for two hours dusting for prints, gathering information, and taking photos of and samples from the victim. A few local police officers roamed the house, more or less there just to make their presence known. They left the big work to the Homicide and CSI units.

Manny tried to stifle a yawn. *Man, am I beat.* They called him very early that morning, and he had come as soon as he could drag himself out of bed. Usually he would have been up by then, but last night he had been worried about Alex. He couldn't help thinking how thin and tired she looked and hadn't been able to fall asleep until 3 a.m. *Well*, he thought, *what better way to wake up in the morning than to the piercing ring of the phone and the announcement of a new victim*, he thought.

"Castillo," a deep voice called out.

Deshawn Freeman, Manny's partner of six years, came sauntering into the room, his tall, muscular body filling the door frame. He smiled, revealing a set of large, beautiful white teeth. Manny was surprised that he still had all of his teeth. Deshawn had played football in college, a very successful defensive line-man who had been given the opportunity to go pro. But Deshawn had gracefully declined. He hailed from a long line of police officers and detectives. Desmond Freeman, his great-grandfather was one of the first black police officers to receive an award for service. The next, his grandfather Cedric Freeman, served thirty years on the force. Then his father, Shawn Freeman, was a highly decorated officer when he retired.

"Hey, Freeman," Manny called back.

He walked over to Deshawn, who was standing back a few feet from the body, and patted him on the shoulder. Manny trusted Deshawn with his life. Deshawn invited Manny to his home more and more over the last few years, and Manny had grown closer to Deshawn's family. Deshawn's wife Muriel was a beautiful blonde woman in her late twenties whom Deshawn had met in college. She was one of the cheerleaders for Deshawn's football team, and he had fallen head over heels for her the first time he saw her. Muriel laughed when

story, and their two children laughed too, even tho

young to know what they were all laughing about.

was four and their daughter, Reagna, was two - bo

of mother and father. Manny smiled as he thought of them laughing

and playing.

"Can you believe it?" Deshawn broke into Manny's thoughts. "Another housewife found dead? This is the fourth in three months," he said, shaking his head in disbelief.

"Same cause of death..." Manny added.

"Yup, same M.O. It seems like it started as consensual sex and ended in strangulation just like the others. But…." He paused for dramatic effect.

Manny knew that face; he had something up his sleeve. That huge smile grew bigger, and Manny thought for a moment that he might rip his cheeks apart one day from smiling so big.

"But what?" Manny prodded.

"But this time he left a calling card," Deshawn said as he walked over to the bed.

Manny noticed for the first time that Deshawn had been holding something in his hand: a blue light. Deshawn turned it on and passed it over the bed, over the victim's body, close to her exposed genitalia. *Semen*, Manny thought, as the blue light exposed a few small splotches of blue-white between her thighs.

"I see," he said.

Manny's stomach flipped with that old feeling of excitement at this find. The last three women they had found had no traces of semen inside them or on their bodies, and there had been no fingerprints left at the scenes. Without DNA it was hard to find a killer. The only thing they had to go on until now was the pattern; sex and strangulation.

49

ere hadn't even been any witnesses, in broad daylight no less. *Damn our bad luck*, Manny thought. *Well, until now I guess.* Manny smiled.

"CSI is going to gather it up now and take it to the lab. We were just waiting until you got here to show you before they took it. We should hopefully have a hit in CODIS in a few hours, God willing." Deshawn smiled again, his bright, big smile.

Manny chuckled a little bit. He just loved his partner's enthusiasm. He hoped they would get a hit off the criminal database, hoped that this DNA had somehow found its way into their system sometime before today. Just then his cell phone started to ring. He picked it up on the third ring.

"Detective Castillo here," he said. Immediately he could tell something was wrong. The tone of her voice seared him like fire. His breath caught in his throat.

"Manny! Thank God! I didn't know what to do, so I called you." Alex's breath came rattling through the phone. He could hear it trembling with every word.

"Alex, what is wrong? What is going on? Are you okay? Where are you?" Manny practically screamed into the phone.

Everyone in the room turned to look at him. He took a deep breath, gathered himself and waved them all off. *Get back to work*, the wave said, *and mind your own damn business.*

"I just got a box delivered to my house, on my front porch, Manny." She paused for a moment as if to let the words sink in. Manny couldn't understand why a simple box delivered to her home was such a big deal. What could be so bad about a box?

"Okay, so tell me what is wrong?" he said trying not to sound condescending.

"The box, Manny. It had dead, black roses in it."

"Wow! OK. That's not what I was expecting to hear," Manny said, becoming a little agitated but confused nonetheless.

"I know, but that wasn't the worst part. There was a note." Alex struggled to get the words out. Clearly she was very upset. At this point, the hair on the back of Manny's neck stood up and a bead of cold sweat ran down his face.

"What did it say?" Manny tried to sound professional, but he was becoming more worried now.

"It said 'I have been watching you.'" Alex didn't speak the words; they escaped her lips like a child's cry. Manny had never heard her this rattled before.

"Okay, I will be there in ten minutes. Don't touch anything!"

CHAPTER TEN

STELLA ADAMS WALKED FROM THE OFFICE ACROSS THE parking lot towards her trusty old yellow beetle bug car. She wore her "Friday outfit" and her "Friday smile." Pulling the scarf tighter around her neck, she wished she had brought her winter coat today. She had opted not to because it made her look like the Michelin Man, and no one is attracted to the Michelin Man. Light flurries of snowflakes danced around her, landing on her curly red hair and on the tip of her freckled button nose. She blew out an exasperated breath up towards her nose where a snowflake had landed and was tickling her.

He watched her from across the street. She wasn't a pretty woman by any means. He didn't like red hair, and she was plump in her little black and white polka dotted dress. Still, he felt a little sad at the fact that he would have to get rid of her. She had been so nice to him when he came for the job. The job required references and a driver's license. He had a fake license made just the week before. He met some weasel in a local bar a year ago who had given him a couple of different fake identities to the tune of three hundred dollars. He hadn't worried about the guy betraying him because as soon as he had the fakes in hand he quickly disposed of the idiot, keeping his money and his real identity safe. He hadn't been able to provide her with any references, though. He told her he had just moved up from down south and didn't have any friends around here yet, and no family back home. She had shown great sympathy for him when he told her and hated to turn him away without giving him a chance. Plus, they really needed some techs at the time, so she penciled in a few names for him. She told her boss she had checked all the references, and he had come back golden. He could tell she was attracted to him. He had caught her staring at him more than a few times, and she had never once mentioned the scar on his face.

The scar had faded over the years but was still very visible. She had tried not to stare, not to let him notice that the scar frightened her a bit. A few weeks later, he told her he had gotten it when he was ten. He told her a horrific tale of a car accident that had scarred his face and ended his parents' lives, leaving him with no living relatives. Little did she know his father had branded him with the scar during one of his many drunken "episodes," as his mother used to call them. From that point on, Stella really liked him, just as he intended. He knew he was the first guy in a while to be kind and give her attention. At first he had only been nice to her to get the job, but over time she had kind of grown on him. He wasn't attracted to her in any way but could feel the desire for attention oozing from her body, so he gave her a little. It could only serve him in a time of need. At least that is what he had thought until now. She held the information that could be his downfall. She knew what he looked like and, more importantly, she knew he had been in the houses of the women that had been found dead.

Stella opened the door to her car and got in. The car sagged with her weight and, had he been close enough, he would have heard it creak in complaint. He knew where she was going. She went there every Friday night. He knew this because on more than one occasion she had tried to get him to go with her. He had politely declined, and she had cheerfully accepted his "rain check," even though he knew she was disappointed every time. After a while, she stopped asking him.

He heard her engine start with a loud grumble, the exhaust pipe coughing white smoke into the frigid air like a tired, old dragon complaining about the winter months. He watched as she slowly pulled out from the parking lot and drove down the street towards the highway. He followed her, careful to stay at least a few car lengths behind her at all times. He couldn't risk her seeing him. Not yet.

They drove for about fifteen minutes down the highway through the evening traffic. He kept her tail lights in his view. He couldn't lose her because he didn't actually know where this place was, he just knew she went there and what it was. He was letting his thoughts drift a bit, wondering what she would feel like in his hands, when Stella's car took a sudden leap from the center lane to the far right lane.

"Shit!" he exclaimed as he pulled the steering wheel to a hard right barely missing the tail end of the car in front of him.

She drove faster now, heading towards the exit for downtown. *I have to pay better attention*, he chastised himself. There would be time for thinking later. He followed her down a few busy side streets. They were in the downtown area now. The lights of businesses, clubs, and restaurants stood out in contrast to the black night sky. Cars whizzed by him, and people walked along the crowded sidewalks, laughing and talking. There were times when he wished he could be "one of them," normal and average - but he knew he was neither average or normal. He was special, his mother had always told him, and his father had left a mark on his face to prove it.

He parked a few cars down from hers. The parking lot was not full, not even close, but he parked on the street so he could have a full visual of the front of the bar. He slumped down slightly and watched as she waited near the entrance. He waited, watching, and true to what she had divulged to him before, three of Stella's friends showed up. They were all laughing and hugged ceremoniously before entering the bar.

He knew he had about three hours to sit back and wait now, according to the weekly routine. Stella had told him of how her friends met her on Fridays. They all "eat a bunch of apps and drink a bunch of drinks, and then they leave me to go home to their families. I stay and have one more with me, myself, and I," she had complained. He remembered feeling a bit bad for her at the time, but now he felt like the luckiest man in the world. He couldn't have planned this any better. So he sat back and relaxed, watching and waiting.

A few hours passed while he watched people come and go through the bar's unmanned front door. The pack of Camels lay in the seat next to him and, just as he thought about reaching for one, he glanced up to see the three women leaving the bar. *Aw, this is it. It's go time.* He forgot the Camels and hefted himself out of his car, closing the door behind him. He didn't bother locking it. He wasn't afraid of it being stolen.

The inside of the bar was dark and reeked of cigarette smoke and alcohol. He enjoyed the smell as he walked deeper into the darkness - the loud din of laughing people filling his head. He saw her in the corner, sitting at a booth all alone. A margarita sat in front of her, a few sips of frozen green liquid missing from the glass. She didn't see him. She wasn't looking around, just sitting there alone listening to the Eagles "Hotel California" drone in the background. He knew what he would say to her, knew how he would act. He had played it out in his mind all day long while he waited for her to get out of work.

"Hey, Stella," he yelled, trying to sound excited, raising his voice over the music and the people.

"Hey, Joe?" She looked up almost as if she were in shock and mouthed the words slightly in disbelief.

For a minute he wondered if she were frightened, if she knew what he had done. Her eyes were wide behind her green tortoise-shell glasses, and her mouth hung slightly open in mid-sentence. His fear was quickly replaced with pleasure as a smile spread across her face. She had a piece of black pepper in between her two front teeth, and he wanted to reach across the table and punch it out of her mouth with his huge fist.

She had called him Joe. Joe, of course, was the name on the license he had given her. He had many others but thought Joe Smith was the easiest to remember. He had to laugh at how generic it sounded, but she hadn't blinked an eye when he introduced himself. His real name was Bobby Benson, Jr., but he hadn't used that name in a very, very long time. Just the thought of it flooded him with hatred and memories that he could not erase, no matter how hard he tried.

"What on earth are you doing here?" she asked him, the not so perfect smile with the black pepper in between her teeth still lingering on her chubby, freckled face. He smiled as he thought what he might be doing to that face later on. *Wait*, he thought, *patience*.

"Where have you been? You haven't been to work in like two weeks. I have been so worried about you. I called the number you put on your application, but it said it wasn't in service. What…." she rambled on peppering him with slurred questions.

He knew it would be like this, and he had all the answers. He just had to wait for her to stop talking. When she had finally finished assaulting him with questions, he began his well-practiced speech.

"I am so sorry you were worried about me." He smiled sweetly. "I tried to call the office a few times, but no one answered. I have been extremely ill. I was in the hospital with the flu. Dehydrated and contagious, you know? And my phone must have gotten disconnected while I was there because I missed a few payments. That is so embarrassing, but I am sure you understand. Anyways, I remembered you asking me to come here with you a few times, and I am feeling better and all. You know I have been thinking about you a lot lately, and…." he paused, waiting for her reaction.

When he paused, her smile broadened and her already ruddy cheeks flooded to a near crimson red. He embarrassed and excited her at the same time. He felt so good right now. He knew he was a nice looking man, even though he looked just like the one man he'd despised his whole life. His father had been good for one thing, making good looking offspring. It had been rumored that his old man had at least five illegitimate children running around. Bobby wasn't sure how true the rumors were, and he never had enough interest to find out.

"You have been thinking of… me?" she stammered.

He was sitting next to her and used this opportunity to move in closer. His skin crawled with disgust. She smelled like Tequila and spices - what kind he wasn't sure - but nonetheless, he could almost taste her breath. He had to suppress the urge to rip her tongue out. He was so close to her now, he could feel the warmth coming off her body. Small beads of sweat were pooling at the very edge of the hairline on her forehead. He thought if he stared long enough he would see one trickle down her face.

"I have…. um, a lot," he managed to choke out and, with great effort, he gently touched her hand. He felt electricity fly from her fingertips. He knew he wouldn't have to explain anymore. He knew he was in from here on out. As he folded her small, chunky hand into his large muscular one, he could feel her sweaty palm pulsing. Her heart was pounding. He wasn't surprised he had this affect on her.

They only sat for ten minutes or so. She was slurring her words, and her eyes were already glossy when he had sat down. When she spilled the last of her drink, he knew she was ready to go.

"So Stella, what are you doing after this?" he asked, leading her towards what he needed her to say. Her eyes widened at the question, and again her cheeks flushed.

"I was just going to go home," she answered, her eyes asking the question before her lips could. "Would, I mean, do you think you would want to, maybe come over for a little while?" she stumbled and stuttered over the words.

Bobby knew she would. She was not accustomed to doing things like this. A thought flashed through his mind; *what if she is still a virgin?* He smiled and had to suck in a breath to keep from laughing out loud at the thought.

"I would love to come over. I will even drive you home in your car so you don't have to worry about coming back to get it," he said.

He had thought this whole plan out. If they left her car at the bar, people would be suspicious a lot sooner than they would by Monday morning when Stella didn't show up for work. He knew she had an excellent record for showing up to work. *Of course she did*, he thought, *she had nothing else to do*.

She smiled at him and gave him her hand. He helped her out of the booth they had been sitting in. She seemed to barely notice that her thick, white thighs were stuck to the seat or the awful ripping sound they made as they peeled away from the plastic. The backs of her legs were red and slightly chafed from sweating and sitting too long. He grinned, thinking that was nothing compared to what he was going to do to her.

CHAPTER ELEVEN

THE NIGHT HAS GOTTEN SO COLD, SHE THOUGHT. SHE could see her breath coming out of her mouth. *I'm smoking*, she thought. She laughed a little and had to catch her balance, on the brink of teetering over. *Oh, man. I'm drunk.* She hoped it wouldn't turn him off. They walked to her car, and she handed him the keys. He let her in on the passenger side, opening the door for her, and helping her in so that she didn't fall. *Oh, he's so sweet, such a gentleman,* she thought. She laid her head back against the seat and closed her eyes. She felt almost giddy with the thought that a guy like Joe was bringing her home. She had never actually had any guy over to her place before, and she certainly hadn't thought she would be his type. She actually didn't feel like she was anyone's type. No one ever asked her out, and she never had the nerve to ask anyone out. She had only been with one other man in her lifetime. She laughed at this thought because, at the time, he hadn't even been a man yet. She was a young girl when he had stolen her life.

They had only known each other for a short while. She had just moved to Tennessee with her family a few months before when her dad's job relocated them. Adjusting to another new school was not easy, especially in high school, and especially being "a nerdy fat girl." She ran into him in the hallway a few times and, after the third time, he started talking to her. It took her by surprise, but she welcomed the contact.

He was a tall scrawny kid with a pimply face and greasy black hair. He smelled of mothballs and Vick's vapor rub. She remembered thinking he must have had to use it a lot at night, and she wasn't sure if he frequented the shower very often. Even still, after awhile she started to like him, and he acted like he really liked her. He wasn't even embarrassed to be seen with her at school. She recalled the last day they were together. They were behind an old barn a few blocks from the high school. He liked to take her there. It was dilapidated and smelled of rotting corn, but she didn't care because she was with him. He had tried to touch her before, to kiss her. She allowed him to caress her large breasts and even put his tongue in her mouth. She remembered his taste, like licorice and cigars. That day was warm and the sun beat down on them. They were lying on a blanket that he brought there the last time they came. She knew why he had brought it, but today she didn't care. Today she wanted it to happen. She had decided last night after he called her and told her to meet him at the barn that she was going to give it to him. She didn't see any reason for waiting until she was married. She knew she wasn't pretty, and she wasn't sure she would ever marry unless she married him. She thought about it a lot. They were only sixteen, but the way she felt about him in such a short time of knowing him made her feel very strongly about the possibility.

She wore her best dress that day...a red and white checkered dress her mom made her. Her mother made all her clothes because it was cheap and, at that time, it was a little hard to find clothes Stella liked that were in her size. He brought a picnic basket and placed it on the blanket. He opened it and showed her the peanut butter and jelly sandwiches he had made for them. She was elated. He had done all of this for her. He had made her favorite sandwiches, and he loved her. She knew he did. He hadn't said it yet, but she knew.

After they ate, they laid back on the blanket, each on their side facing one another. He had already taken his shirt off. She was worried about him getting a sunburn. He was so pale and thin. She didn't think his mother ever fed him. He smiled at her as he ran his finger down the line of her cleavage playfully. She giggled at this. She liked the way he touched her. He kissed her then, lightly on one cheek then on the other. Then he kissed her lips. *He tastes like peanut butter, yummy*, she thought. She let him roll his tongue inside her mouth. Her tongue felt good playing with his. She felt a tingle down below. She was unsure of herself. Was she supposed to feel that? She had never felt that before. As if reading her mind, he slipped his hand up her dress and gently touched her down there. Her body trembled as he touched her, and she felt a rush of warmth below. She moaned as he moved his hand on her and then slid his finger into her. She gasped in surprise.

Just when she thought she was ready, she felt a deep feeling of guilt rush through her like a tidal wave. *Oh my god, I am not supposed to be doing this,* she thought. Her mother would kill her if she knew what she was doing. She would know. She would see it on her face when she got home. She would smell it on her. She had turned to tell him she had changed her mind and that she didn't feel comfortable doing this when she realized he was on top of her moving her panties to the side. Before she even knew what was happening he was inside her. She screamed, no, no, no, but he covered her mouth. It hurt so badly. What was he doing to her? *Why?* She begged him to stop but he just kept going. His face was red, and his forehead and back were covered in sweat. She couldn't believe this was happening to her. She looked into his face. It was twisted and mangled looking, different from the one she knew so well before. *Why*? His hand was covering her mouth, pushing so hard she could barely breathe. *I can't breathe,* she thought, her mind closing in on her. She squeezed her eyes shut, trying to make the memory go away. It felt so real; the pain down below, searing heat, ripping pain. The pressure from his hand over her mouth was suffocating, she could barely breathe. She opened her eyes and, for a split second, was even more confused than before. That is when she saw him, really saw him. His face was perverse, a mixture of anger and pleasure, and she could feel him ripping her apart. He was huge and the sweat dripped from his body. She cried out in recognition.

"Joe, what the hell?" she screamed.

He stopped for a second, a confused look on his face. She was as confused as he looked. What had happened? How had she gotten here? She started to open her mouth to ask him but looked at him and closed her mouth. Anger had replaced confusion and his face flushed bright red. Stella's eyes were still trying to adjust but she knew the flash of hatred she saw gleam in his eyes before what came next.

He raised his fist and punched her hard. The sting was not muffled by the loads of alcohol in her system. It burned her cheek, and she tasted the blood in her mouth. Her eyes widened in shock and disbelief. She was about to scream at him again when his other fist slammed her in the face, rocking her to the other side. The pain scorched her cheek like a hot coal, and she felt as if she would throw up. White flecks of light danced around her as she tried to figure out where she was. She locked her eyes on the familiar Hello Kitty lampshade and realized they were in her room, on her bed. *Oh my god*, she shuddered at the thought. He was raping her in her own bed. She would never be able to sleep here again. She had to do something, anything. She thought she might try pleading with him.

"Joe, please listen," she started, and again another fist brought her to silence.

Why is he doing this? She thought. This time she felt something sharp floating around in her mouth. He must have knocked out one of her teeth. She instinctively tried to move her right hand toward her mouth to pick it out but realized she couldn't move either arm. They were tied to the posts of her canopy bed. *My scarves*, she thought. He used her own scarves to tie her to her own bed. The bile was sitting just below her throat now, threatening to escape. She had to swallow to keep it down.

Another fist came, hitting her square in the left eye. She thought her eye might pop right out of its socket from the impact. Her arm twisted and pulled, trying to reach out and touch the eye that she could feel closing up almost instantly. Again, she tasted blood. More blood this time, like thick iron water filling her mouth. She gagged as vomit replaced the taste of blood and attempted to spit it out. She choked on it. It sputtered out of her mouth as she tried to cry out. She could see the mixture of vomit and blood as it exploded from her mouth. It was full of blood, a lot of blood. *Oh God, please help me.* She could feel her head spinning and her eyes rolling into the back of her head. No, she couldn't pass out right now. She couldn't. She had to fight some-how, someway. She hadn't fought the first time this had happened to her, but she sure as hell was going to find a way to fight this time. She tried desperately to open her swollen eyes, searching for something, anything, she could use against him. He hit her again. She could tell he knew what she was doing, why she was looking around. She spat at him, the blood hitting his face. He was no longer handsome to her. His face had become a warped mass of insanity. He laughed as the blood hit his face, spraying a crimson pattern across his forehead, cheeks, and scar. *Oh god*, she whined underneath him...the scar on his face. Now she doubted the story he had told her. Now she doubted everything. Just as she was wondering if he was going to hit her again, she felt it....his hands around her throat. *Oh no, oh no, please*, she begged inside her head. She tried to get his attention, but realized no sound was coming from her mouth except for a gurgling hiccup of blood and breath. Stella knew what was happening but couldn't do anything about it. She kicked and squirmed underneath him but his weight was unbearable. He was so strong, his hands around her neck like a vice closing around her vulnerable airway. This time she heard something else come from her mouth, a gasp, a choke, another gurgle. *Please, no, this is it*, she thought. She tried one last time to suck in a breath, any breath, but the darkness took her. It came slowly like some far away spot in the sky. It grew bigger and bigger, a black hole growing, churning, coming for her like a freight train roaring through her head. Finally, there was nothing else, no pain, no sound, no fear. The blackness was all that was left.

CHAPTER TWELVE

HE SAT ON THE FLOOR NEXT TO HER FOR A WHILE, HIS breath slowing as he watched her. She was so still now. She had put up quite a fight. He was glad that at the last minute he found her scarves and decided to tie her up to that little princess bed she had in her room. He hadn't expected her to even wake up, but what a thrill it was to see her struggle. The excitement he felt when he had looked into her wild eyes was better than getting off. *Their eyes were always wild at the end, like a trapped animal*, he thought. Once they realized what was happening to them, and that they couldn't do anything about it, the eyes shifted from wild to bewildered.

He hadn't meant to have sex with her, he wasn't even attracted to her. He was actually repulsed by her at the bar, with her pepper teeth and sweaty forehead. But in the car, after she passed out, she had begun to moan. He thought she might be having some sex dream, and it made him horny. Why not? It had been two weeks since he had had sex with anyone besides himself. It just made the kill more intoxicating.

His first kill was at the age of fifteen. It was different than any other since because he had loved her. Bobby hadn't wanted to kill her, but she told him she didn't want him anymore - that she had someone else, someone better. How could he let someone else have her? He could still smell her hair, like sunflowers and honey. He recalled her lips. They were slightly thin lips that always seemed to be a little chapped, but he never minded kissing them. To him they always felt soft. Her eyes were ice blue, and he remembered spending hours staring into them. Her eyes had quieted him; made him forget his painful existence, if only for a little while. Eyes that made him feel safe...blue pools of water swallowing him. That was, until the day she told him she didn't want him around her anymore.

He hadn't been home for a few days, sleeping in fields and on park benches. He was very thin for his large frame back then. Even at fifteen he was already over six feet tall. He had gone to see her in the school yard like he had every school day for the last year. He didn't go to her school. In fact, he didn't go to school at all since his mother died when he was seven. He didn't care to go to school, and his deadbeat father was locked away. The different sets of foster parents tried for many years to make him go, but once he hit his teenage years he just kept running away. They had all eventually given up on him.

She hadn't smiled at him that day like she usually did when she came over to the fence. She ran over to him, all her friends watching, her eyebrows furrowed. He wondered what was wrong with her. A small tear ran down her dirty cheek, making a clean path of skin that only he would have noticed. Before he could ask her, she blurted out, "I hate you, Bobby Benson, and I never want to see you again! I… I…I found someone else." With that, she turned and ran away. She ran back to her friends, and he watched as they encircled her and patted her on the back. It looked like they were congratulating her. At first he didn't move, caught up in confusion and anger. Had she really just said that? Maybe he heard her wrong. But he couldn't deny what she had just screamed at him, *I hate you Bobby Benson. I hate you. I hate you.* The words echoed through his ears like the bellow of the church bell used to when he was young. He had hated the sound of that damn church bell, but his mother insisted on bringing him there every Sunday for service. It seemed that they would ring that church bell from the moment they drove up until the moment the preacher started talking. He couldn't stand it.

Then, with her words still ringing, he grabbed his ears and held on tight. He knew what would come next...the blackness, the voice, the evil. He had to get out of there. He turned and ran down the road. He ran until he couldn't run anymore. He ran until his breath was caught in his chest and his sides ached like someone was stabbing him. He kept running until he reached the corn fields where they used to play hide and seek. ***You gonna let her talk to you like that, boy?*** *Oh no*, he thought. The evil was here, and it was speaking to him. *No*, he thought, *it can't be here. I ran away. I ran so hard away from it. It can't be talking to me right now.* ***Oh yes, I am here, boy. I can see you, you little shit. I heard the whole thing. I heard what that little bitch said to you, and now I am asking you.....are you gonna let her get away with THAT?????*** The evil got louder and louder. He only knew one way to silence the evil, and that was to do what it told him to do. He didn't want to. Lord, he didn't want to. But he knew if he didn't, the evil would keep haunting him until he got sick, real sick. So, he sat down in the cornfield and waited for it to get dark.

Once it was dark, he walked slowly to her house. She lived in a run down house a few miles out of town. The house was falling apart, set off of a dirt road that was hardly ever traveled. He wasn't worried about being seen. The evil had told him that it would watch over him, take care of him, and keep him safe. It was the first week of June, and the hot southern days were beginning to take over. School would be out soon. He knew because she had told him. The night sky was clear and the stars shone brightly, lighting his way to her. He walked into her yard and sat down behind one of the few bushes that remained there. Her father had once been a prosperous farmer, but since he had taken up the bottle a few years back, the fields were overgrown with weeds and no crops grew. He wouldn't have to wait for too long. Bobby knew her father would be passed out soon in his chair in front of the television that blared clearly through the open windows. Her old man was a lot like his own father, and that was what had brought them so close together in the first place. It was before dawn the first day they met when she had seen him standing in her field crying. She came to him curiously, too young to be cautious or scared. He had turned away, embarrassed and angry.

"Hey, boy. What's wrong?" she had asked, obviously not afraid of him even though he stood almost a foot above her.

She was only thirteen then, but her thin body was beginning to develop. He could see small breasts poking out from her white night-gown. He remembered thinking she had probably already gotten her menstrual cycle and had felt a tingling sensation in his loins. He was fourteen then, and standing there so close to her, he could feel himself getting hard. Even through the sadness and anger he was feeling at that moment, she still touched him deeply the first time he had laid eyes on her.

"Nothing," he answered, surprised at himself.

He hadn't meant to even speak to her. He thought about running away as soon as he saw her, but when he turned to look her way, her icy blue eyes held him there. His feet felt as if they were cast in stone. That is when he noticed the fading bruise on her left cheek. It was already turning a pale yellow color, but he had been on the receiving end of enough bruises in his lifetime to know what it was.

"Yeah, I do a lot of nothin' out here, too," she said.

He actually managed half a smile for her. He hadn't smiled in almost a year, yet there was something about this young little thing. She looked like an angel with her straggly long black hair and dirty white nightdress. Her feet were bare, caked with crusty old dirt. It looked like she had been beaten on her legs as well. She had many bruises and scabs on her knees and legs. He felt a deep shooting pain for her in the pit of his stomach. He wasn't sure who was beating her, but he could guess. It was a small southern town and word got around fast. Just like his own father, hers was the subject of many gossip sessions. He knew her mother was still around, unlike his own. He doubted she was a 'stand up to your man' kind of woman, though. She was probably huddled in a closet somewhere, hiding from her husband, or hunched quietly at his side waiting for him to bark orders at her. That was how Bobby's mother had been when his father was around. When his father was gone, cheating or at the local bar, she was a much different woman. She sang a lot. Her voice was beautiful, flowing like liquid silk from her lips. Sometimes, if he was lucky, she would sing him a bedtime song. But most of the time she would keep to herself. She was a sad, quiet woman. Bobby resented her for not standing up to his father, for not taking him and leaving his father and the abuse they both suffered from him.

"I'm Angela," she said. He felt his stomach flip when she said her name. *Angela, like "angel"*, he had thought. He knew right then and there she would be his.

He thought of all this as he sat outside of her house. It hurt deeply to remember the good things about her, especially when he remembered what he was there to do. It had been two hours since he had hidden behind the bush, and all the lights in the house had gone black. He saw the crooked tree that he climbed so many times to get to her bedroom window. He remembered all too well the first night he climbed up to see her, and she let him in wearing nothing but what God had given her. She let him take her virginity that night. He hadn't asked, but she knew he wanted to. Even though she was only fourteen at the time, and they had only known each other for a year, he felt it was right and so did she. She cried that night, not in pain, but happiness she told him. She loved him, and he loved her. A tree branch stabbed at his face. *Pay attention*, he chastised himself. Her window was open like it always was. She only kept it closed during the winter time. He climbed in quietly and effortlessly. He had done this a million times.

He could see her shadow, a small lump in the bed. Her body moved up and down as she breathed in a deep sleep. *I don't have to do this. I love her.* **She doesn't love you anymore. She has found someone else to take your place, you loser. Do it. Do it now, or you will pay. You will have to see her with someone else. You will have to watch them together, seeing her happier than she ever was with you. She belongs to you. If you can't have her, no one can!** The evil yelled at him, causing him to lose his balance. He caught himself just in time. He almost knocked something off of her dresser. That would surely wake her up. He was angry again. *How could she find someone else?* She had told him she loved him. He moved over to the bed. He gently removed the pillow from under her head, careful not to wake her. He smelled the pillow. It smelled just like her hair, sunflowers and honey. After a moment of watching her sleep, he placed it over her face and pushed down as hard as he could.

At fifteen he had shot up over six feet and weighed almost two hundred and twenty pounds now, muscular from working different odd jobs as a laborer. She was so small and light that there was barely any strength behind her struggle. She only lasted a few minutes, her feet and arms flailing less and less. She finally went limp. He watched her chest for any signs of breath but she lay so still. When he removed the pillow to look at her face once more, tears rolled down his face.

He had been caught a few days later trying to cross the state line. The police knew it was him. Her father had told them about him, said he had been the father of Angela's unborn baby. They charged Bobby with first degree murder and second degree manslaughter and locked him up in juvenile detention. They released him on his twentieth birthday, but to this day he still felt imprisoned. He had never known she was carrying his baby. He had never known that her father had forced her to say those words to him that day and was going to make her give up the baby. Had he known those things maybe it would have all been so different, maybe.....

"Shit!" he exclaimed.

The cigarette he had been smoking burned between his fingertips. He jumped, shaken from his memory by the burning flesh on his fingers. He threw the cigarette away from him in anger onto the bedroom floor. Just then two separate swirls of smoke caught his eye for a moment. He watched as they ascended towards the ceiling, shifting sideways and up like a winding dance between two lovers. He watched them for a moment before turning his attention back to Stella. Her Hello Kitty alarm clock told him it was four a.m., yet he wasn't tired. He had been here for three hours. As he wiped his eyes of memories and fresh tears, he realized how nice it had felt to kill Stella. He thought that after doing this for so long he might get tired or bored of it, but that simply wasn't the case. Each time was like the first, just as exciting, just as thrilling. He may have even experienced the exact opposite effect. He may actually be enjoying it more and more. He smiled at the thought. He was just practicing with all of these women, finding out what worked best, getting used to the feel, getting his feet wet. He was training for the big day when he could get to her. He had to do it soon, though. He thought he might be getting sloppy recently, and maybe the cops were gaining on him. He couldn't risk being caught before he had his chance with her. It just might kill him.

CHAPTER THIRTEEN

ALEX AWOKE WITH A START. SHE SAT STRAIGHT UP IN BED, gasping for air. Her body was sweaty and shaky. Her heart pounded in her chest, and her head throbbed. She looked around, the dim light of dawn barely lighting the room for her to see. She reached over and turned on her bedside lamp. It cast a comforting glow throughout her bedroom. She saw a light shining beneath her doorway and, for a split second, wondered what Abuela was doing up so early in the morning. Then, with a pang of sadness, she realized it wasn't Abuela. It was Manny. He had slept over last night because she had been terrified by the note from her "secret admirer." She thought she could smell coffee trying to lure her out of bed. She smiled at the thought of Manny stumbling around in her kitchen looking for this or that. He had really helped her out yesterday. He made a few phone calls to the police station, and the CSI unit had come and taken away her package. She had to explain how the white envelope had gotten blood on it, and that it was her blood there. They had taken the box, the UPS note, a cotton swab of DNA from her cheek to match her DNA with that of the blood on the envelope, and the little white envelope containing the letter. *The*

letter, she thought. She had been so scared and angry since she had read it. Why would anyone want to send her something like that, and who exactly had been watching her? She had gone over and over it with Manny yesterday at the diner. He had insisted on taking her to dinner to get her out of the house. He told her that she had spent enough time holed up in the house when her grandmother had died. He didn't want her doing it again just because there might be some crazed lunatic out there watching her. He had smiled his lovely smile and promised she would be safe with him. She knew she would. She always felt safe with him. It continued to amaze her how comfortable she felt around him, how peaceful. Still she fought back the fear, remembering the whole scene from yesterday all over again. She had seen plenty of psychotic people in her line of work - from the highly functioning who came to her "just to talk" to the schizophrenic murderers that she helped Manny, Deshawn and the Newbury Police Department catch. She had seen gruesome murder scenes. She had heard graphic recounts of vicious murders, including the guy who had cooked and eaten his victims saying that "their skin had tasted better than bacon". But she had never felt fear like she did now. The worst part was the unknown - not knowing who was out there, what they were capable of, and why they were targeting *her*. CSI called Manny around seven that night to let him know that they found three sets of fingerprints on the box... Alex's, the UPS guy's, and those of the flower shop worker. Also, only her prints and the prints of the flower shop worker had been found on the white envelope. She shook her head trying to jostle the thoughts right out of her mind. She stood from the bed, pulled up the sheets and down comforter, and fluffed her pillow. She put on her blue fuzzy slippers, her matching blue terry cloth housecoat, and walked out of her bedroom. Shuffling down the hall she listened to the scuffling sound her slippers made on the hardwood floors. Sitting there on the couch was Manny and on his lap was Elefantito, purring in all his glory. Manny patted the cat's head lightly and watched out the bay window as the sun began to peak, spilling splendid rays of sunshine into Alex's living room. As she came into the room, he turned to greet her.

"Hey there, sleepyhead. How are you this morning?" his smile as radiant as the sunlight that splashed in her face. Alex grinned. His hair was a mess from sleeping and his clothes were wrinkled, but he still was so easy on the eyes.

"Hey there, bedhead," she teased. "I guess I am doing alright."

Manny blushed at the name-calling, reaching up to run his fingers through his thick, black hair, taming it only slightly. He looked like a little boy awakened from a sound sleep.

"Have you slept at all?" she asked. Alex felt bad that he had slept on the couch but she couldn't bring herself to let him sleep in Abuela's room, and she certainly was not letting him into her bed.

"Yeah, I slept. I never sleep late, though. You should know that." She did know that, remembering a few very early morning phone calls that had come before her five a.m. alarm clock had a chance to ring. She studied his handsome face, looking for something, anything that would give away what had kept him up last night. She could tell he hadn't slept much. Was it the couch that she knew was too small for his large body, or the fact that he knew someone was out there watching her?She wasn't sure.

"So, what do you think about the present I got?" she asked. He sighed a bit, and thought for a minute.

"Well, I think it is quite interesting, to say the least." He answered, rubbing his chin with its colony of little stubby hairs that had moved in overnight. He hadn't had any of his things, hadn't been prepared to stay with her last night. But it hadn't deterred him from staying. She loved that about him. He was willing to do just about anything for her. He was her best friend, her only friend.

"Yeah, I have been thinking the same thing. I have been wondering if it might be one of my patients." She threw it out there again, knowing they had just discussed that possibility over dinner last night.

"What I want you to do is make a list of your patients. They will be, of course, male, most likely caucasion, ages twenty to forty to start. I want you to focus on the ones with schizophrenic and psychotic behaviors, especially obsessive or obsessive compulsive disorders. Any and all with hypersexualized behaviors. Be sure to include any that you think might have any ill feelings towards you. Once you have the list we will go over it. I am sure some of the people you come up with will be in jail now, so we will be able to count them out. Of course, there is always the possibility that it is someone you don't know," he said.

Alex visibly shuddered at the thought. He felt awful seeing her like this. He was hoping that it might be one of her patients and not someone she didn't know. If it were someone she didn't know, they were going to have a very difficult time tracking and catching him.

"Okay, I will put together a list at work today," she said.

"Oh, and by the way, we have another body in the housewife murders."

"Really?" she asked. She had known they would, from what she had seen before. This guy wasn't going to quit killing.

"Yeah, so it looks like we're gonna need your famous profiling again. Oh, and guess what? This time your killer got sloppy. He left some evidence behind," Manny said, smiling. Alex smiled back. It was always a good thing when they had actual physical evidence.

"As always, it will be my pleasure to solve your case, Detective Castillo," she smiled.

We are back in the game, she thought. They loved challenging each other on each case, seeing who could catch the killer. A little friendly competition never hurt anyone. He laughed out loud, a deep, robust laugh. He hadn't laughed like that in a while. She soaked it up. She loved to see him happy.

"Well, Dr. Aguilar, I guess you and I will be spending a little more time together." A coy smile formed across Manny's face. "I couldn't ask for anything better for Christmas."

CHAPTER FOURTEEN

HE SAT QUIETLY AT THEIR BEDROOM DOOR, NEITHER ONE of them even noticing him there. The candle lit the room, and all he could smell was the whiskey. Every night it was the same. He would scream at her, and she would cry to him. The slap stung him, even though it never touched his face. He reached up and felt the scar that ran from the top of his scalp to the line of his jaw. Why couldn't he just leave her alone? Why wouldn't she leave him?

He had heard the old ladies at the drugstore talking about it one day. They thought he might have some kind of spell on her, what with her staying with him even though he beat her all the time. "And what about the boy?" they had said. She was teaching him that it was okay to hurt a woman.

Bobby shivered even though it wasn't cold. It was late July, and the house was sweltering hot. Sweat ran down his face and into his eyes. He was only nine then, much larger than most boys his age, but no match for his drunken father. He would though, one day, show him what is was like to get beat on. One day he would save his mother from this, take her away, and give her the life she deserved.

He could see the blood trickle down from the corner of her mouth. He could see the red hand print the slap had left on her cheek. He could see her beautiful green eyes pleading with his father, the right one already swelling shut. His father was hulking above her. She had backed herself into a corner with no more room to run. He grabbed her by the throat and lifted her off the ground with one hand. He could hear his mother gasping for air. His father was so strong and she was such a small woman, frail from years of not taking care of herself, years of neglect. Her eyes bulged out of her head. He held her off the ground sliding her along the wall. "You are a whore," was all he kept saying to her, over and over. What was he doing? Bobby watched his father slide his mother into the frame of the bedroom window. He let go of her throat, her bare feet thudding as they hit the floor. His mother grasped at her own neck trying to catch her breath. She sounded as if she were having an asthma attack to Bobby, even though he knew she didn't have asthma. His father kept saying it; "whore" - chanting it. He had said it to her many times before, even though Bobby had no idea why. His mother was always home. When would she have had the time to sneak out on his father?

Just then, his father stopped chanting. Bobby's head snapped up as he could almost hear it at that second - something exploding inside his father's head. The veins in his father's neck bulged, and his face was bright red. That is when he did it. Bobby's father pushed his mother with all his might. Bobby watched, unable to move, unable to scream, frozen in fear. He watched as his mother's body folded into the window, heard the crash of the glass as it shattered with her weight and a blood curdling scream reached his ears. Then, as quickly as it happened, it was over. There was silence. Bobby stood there in the doorway, mouth gaping in a silent cry, blurry eyes full of tears. After a moment, Bobby's eyes focused and he saw his father, staring straight

at him. Yet, it wasn't his father, it was some kind of monster. Bobby ran.
He ran down the stairs and out the front door. He ran and ran.

After a few hours of hiding behind the shed, he came around to
see his mother. He knew she was dead, but he had to see her. She had
never even reached the ground. She stopped short, impaled, hanging
from one of the posts of the fence his father had put up a few years ago
during one of his sober moments. It stuck out of her chest, painted in
her blood. Her body was limp. Her head fell backwards, hanging,
glass caught in her dirty blonde curls. It was quiet out. Only the song
of crickets and an unfamiliar sound came to his ears. He could hear the
noise, like a single raindrop hitting a tin roof. Just beneath his mother
was a metal pail turned upside down; her blood dripped onto the pail.
"Thud, thud, thud." None of that scared Bobby. What scared him was
her eyes. Her eyes were open, and they were looking straight at him.
They were still green like he remembered, but something had changed…
they were empty. He could not move. All he could do was scream; he
screamed and screamed and screamed…………

Bobby woke himself up screaming. He was drenched in sweat.
He reached over and turned on the lamp beside his bed. It cast an
eerie glow in the aftermath of the dream. His breath came in spurts,
burning in his throat and chest. He fumbled around on the nightstand
trying to find the bottle. He grabbed it and opened it. He hadn't taken
the Lorazepam in a while, but now he needed it. *That must be why the*
dreams are back, he thought. He swallowed a pill and replaced the cap.
I know, I know. I am not supposed to mix it with alcohol, he whined
to the air. He wiped the tears from his eyes and stood up to change
his sweat-soaked t-shirt. He was overwhelmed with feelings. He felt
small and helpless, like he was nine years old again. He was scared.
He looked around his room for a minute to make sure he was really
awake and in the present. He wanted to make sure his father was not

around, even though he had watched the police come that night and take his father away, kicking and screaming. Then they took Bobby to his first foster home. Still, after all these years, he felt his father's looming presence. He was still gripped with fear and anger at the very thought of him. ***You shoulda killed him when you had the chance, you weak little shit.*** The evil was there, it had always been there, hiding, lurking in the dark recesses of his warped mind. He smiled as the Lorazepam kicked in. His eyes grew heavy. He walked back over to the bed and laid down. *Come on evil*, he thought. *I cannot fight you now. Just come on, do what you are going to do.* The darkness came, swallowing him, enshrouding him, and he welcomed it. Bobby closed his eyes.

CHAPTER FIFTEEN

ALEX SAT WITH MANNY AT HIS DESK GOING OVER THE pictures from the last crime scene. They were almost identical to the other two crime scenes she just surveyed. All the women had been found in their own bedrooms raped and strangled in their own beds. Alex shuddered at the thought. This never got any easier for her. She always tried to put her personal feelings aside when working on a case, but at times like these when she had to comb through pictures and think of the murder victims, she wondered why she did this for a living.

"Well, from what I can tell, this guy has some real pent up hatred and aggression towards women. I would guess that he at least had some kind of an estranged relationship with his own mother. He might have been beaten or sexually abused as a child, or maybe both." Alex shook her head.

She looked tired and worn out. Manny watched her strained face as she scanned the photos. He put his hand gently on her shoulder.

"Are you okay, Alex?" he asked, a deep furrow in his brow.

"I'm fine. Just a little tired," she sighed.

"Bad dreams again?" he asked.

Manny knew better than to probe because she usually just shrugged him off. But today she looked especially worried.

"Yeah." Her eyes glazed over a bit and she turned her head away from him.

He watched her for a moment, wondering if he could get her to talk about it. He figured the direct approach would probably work best.

"Wanna talk about it?" he tried.

"Um, no, and don't try to use that psychology stuff on me either. Remember, I am the one with the degree." She smiled half heartedly.

The phone on Manny's desk rang, making Alex jump. Manny grabbed her shoulder again to steady and calm her before picking up the phone. He waited until Alex gave him a "thumbs up" to signal that she was OK before answering.

"Detective Castillo here," Manny said into the phone. There was a pause as he listened to whomever was on the other end of the line. "I see." He sounded a little disappointed. *Bad news*, Alex figured. A few moments passed, then Manny hung up the phone.

"Well, no hit in CODIS for the DNA left behind." His face grew very long. She knew he was upset.

"Well, back to square one. We just have to go with what we do know," she said, trying to sound positive. He looked at her gratefully. He knew he could always count on her.

"So, what we have is probably a large male, most likely Caucasian who, what did you say, probably hates his momma and is a sexual deviant who likes to strangle women?" Manny scribbled on a pad of yellow paper as he spoke. His tone was deflated, a sound Alex was not used to hearing from Manny's lips.

"And no witnesses at any of the crime scenes that might have seen anything….." Alex began, when she was cut off by Deshawn who came barreling into the office. He was out of breath, his famous smile already lighting up his face. Manny stopped him mid-bounce.

"I am afraid I am about to ruin your day, Freeman," he said.

"Well you can try." Deshawn challenged.

"There was no hit on the DNA." Manny paused, waiting for Deshawn to show his disappointment. When Deshawn's big smile didn't budge, Manny said, "Okay now, your turn. Why so happy?"

"I thought you'd never ask," Deshawn teased. "We found another vic."

"And you are happy about that?" Alex asked, astonished at his excitement. She knew he loved his job but, man, that was downright cold.

"Not happy we found a vic, Dr. Aguilar," Deshawn corrected. Alex smiled a little. She had known Deshawn as long as Manny had, even had dinner at his house a few times, but he still insisted on calling her Dr. Aguilar.

"Happy that we found a piece of evidence. That little bastard is getting careless. Oh man, Dr. Aguilar, sorry for the potty mouth," Deshawn smiled sheepishly. Alex laughed at his use of children's slang.

"That's okay, Deshawn. At least, don't do it again," she chided, teasingly.

"Okay, spit it out," Manny said. He wanted to know everything: the victim, the time, the M.O., and, most of all, the evidence.

CHAPTER SIXTEEN

BOBBY STOOD BEHIND ALEX'S HOUSE IN THE BACKYARD. Even though it was bitterly cold, sweat ran down his face and arms, turning icy as it stalled in the small of his back. He couldn't believe he was standing here doing this, in broad daylight. *I'm crazy,* he thought. But the evil had told him it would be okay. The evil had told him that Alex wouldn't be there. The evil had taken him over.

He stared at the cat sitting in Alex's bedroom window, its body pressed up against the screen trying to soak up the heat from the little bit of sunshine that poked in and out of the clouds. The weatherman said it was going to possibly snow today, and Bobby's breath escaped in plumes of smoke from his dry mouth.

Bobby walked over to the window, carrying the white plastic lawn chair he found on the back porch. He placed it under the window and carefully stood on it. It wobbled in protest under his weight. He wore his thick, black leather gloves, and they made it slightly difficult to pull at the screen. The cat jumped out of the window sill at the sight of him. *Scaredy cat,* he laughed. The screen popped as it loosened under his grip, and he slid it out of its frame, careful not to rip it or bend the flimsy metal around it. He laid it against the side of the house and climbed inside.

He landed inside what he quickly realized was Alex's bedroom and grew excited as he looked around at all her things. A queen sized bed with a down comforter and large downy pillows where she laid her head at night invited him to picture her lying there. He closed his eyes and took in a deep breath, smelling her. A familiar scent filled his nostrils, what was it…..*sunflowers…?* His eyes opened in recognition, and he reeled as he caught his own reflection in her dresser mirror. *Damn, that scared me.* He breathed heavily for a moment, his heart pounding. *Scaredy cat,* he thought again after regaining his composure, and giggled with relief and exhilaration.

He went to her dresser drawers and opened one up. He carefully looked through the drawer, not sure exactly what he was searching for, just elated at being there at that moment. He saw some of her panties folded neatly and placed to one side. He picked the top pair up and smelled them. They smelled wonderful. Goosebumps covered his flesh instantly. He stuffed the pair of panties into his coat pocket and closed the dresser drawer. **Come on now, numbnuts, do what you came to do and get out of here.** The evil cursed at him. He obediently turned and walked out of her room.

"Here, kitty, kitty," he called in his sweetest, softest tone. He wasn't sure where the cat had run off to, but he needed to find it.

"Here, kitty, kitty. Where are you, you little piece of shit?" Bobby coaxed in a calm, soothing voice.

He heard a meow coming from another room. He walked down the hallway into the kitchen and looked around. His eyes fell on the pictures that were taped to the refrigerator. *Alex,* he thought. There was a picture of her with an old woman. He knew that was the grandmother. Another picture showed Alex at her graduation with her cap and gown, smiling brightly, holding up her diploma. His lips curled into a smile. A chuckle escaped his lips. Then his brow tightened, pulling his eyebrows together into a deep frown. He saw Alex with Manny. They were standing, cheek to cheek, smiling and laughing. The picture caught their eyes glowing. The picture next to that one must have been taken at the same time, but this one showed them in a different pose. Alex smiled at the camera, a thumb held up in approval. Manny was looking right at her, almost unaware of the camera. It caught Manny's eyes staring at Alex, admiring her, loving her. Bobby was infuriated at that picture. He ripped it off the refrigerator and stuffed it into his pocket, shoving it down deep next to the panties.

He turned to finish his business there. He needed to find the damn cat. He was agitated now, and he could take it out on the stupid thing.

"Here, kitty, kitty. Where are you?" he whispered.

Another meow turned his head toward the living room. The fat tiger cat was laying on the couch staring at him with wide eyes. He walked slowly over to it and patted it on its head.

"Pretty kitty," he sang.

The cat looked at him, unaware of what was about to happen. Just then Bobby's other hand shot out and grabbed the cat by the throat. The cat growled and writhed in his grasp, clawing at him, trying to break free. Low guttural meows gurgled from its open mouth. Bobby watched it for a while. He had never been allowed to have any animals when he was young. He watched as its fangs glistened in the sunlight, wet with saliva, its red tongue caught in mid hiss. In one swift motion the cat was quiet, hanging limp in Bobby's hands. Bobby liked the feeling of the frail bones and the sound they made as they snapped in his large hands. He held the cat for a few moments, wondering what Alex would think of her precious kitty when she found it. He reached into his other pocket with his free hand and pulled out a familiar winter scarf, pink and embroidered with a Hello Kitty design. *How ironic*, he laughed. He wondered if anyone would get the joke. He walked back to the bathroom, whistling a happy little tune, and finished what he came to do.

CHAPTER SEVENTEEN

THEY ALL RODE TO STELLA'S PLACE TOGETHER; MANNY driving, Alex riding shotgun, and Deshawn in the back telling them about last weekend's visit with his in-laws. Alex liked listening to him talk. He was so animated. This story was a particularly funny one, especially when he got to the part about how little Reagan had peed all over her grandpappy's leg. They were in the process of potty training her, he had said, but hadn't really had a lot of luck with it yet. No kidding, Manny had said. They had all laughed at that.

A few minutes later they pulled up to a small set of apartments. It was swarming with police cruisers, yellow police tape, the coroner's van, and, of course, more than a few of the local news stations' vans. They had all gotten used to this kind of traveling circus. Manny pulled the undercover car up past a few marked police cars and parked next to the coroner's van. Alex hated seeing it here. It only ever meant one thing.

They got out of the car just as a slew of reporters rushed at them. Deshawn smiled his great big smile as they headed toward the trio, which excited the reporters. They thought for sure he would be the one to talk to.

"No comment, thank you," he said politely as Manny grabbed Alex's arm, ushering her into the hallway of the apartment building. Deshawn followed closely behind, shooing away reporters buzzing about him like an angry swarm of bees.

"Good Lord," he gasped. "Don't those damned people have anything else to do besides hanging around like leeches trying to suck the blood out of us?" Deshawn asked, wiping a few beads of sweat from his forehead. They looked at him to make sure he was okay.

"You gonna make it, Freeman?" Manny teased.

"I dunno, but if I don't, just tell my wife and kids that I did my best." He laughed.

Manny looked at him and shook his head. Deshawn liked to joke a lot, but Manny never liked to joke about the "tell my wife and kids" speech. He never wanted to have to tell Deshawn's wife and kids anything except "thanks for the BBQ, the food was great." Deshawn knew the look. He just shrugged at Manny and looked at Alex as if asking for a little help.

"Uh uh, Deshawn, you got this one all on your own." She said, shaking her head.

Manny turned and walked down to the end of the hallway. The last door on the left was open, a uniformed police officer posted there. Manny flashed his badge at the police officer and motioned to Alex and Deshawn as if to say "they're with me." The uniform nodded and let them into the apartment, his face expressionless. *He must have had a long night*, Alex thought as they went inside.

Manny looked around and saw the familiar faces of the CSI gang. Some smiled at him as he walked in. A few looked surprised when they saw Alex lagging behind. One guy she knew a little from the lab yelled out, "Hey, Dr. Aguilar. How are you doing? Long time no see." Alex smiled and put her hand up in a wave. She didn't exactly feel like being chummy today, but she didn't want to be rude either.

Manny led them into the back bedroom. The curtains had been drawn to keep out peeping eyes and flashing cameras. Only a single Hello Kitty lamp lit the room. Everything in there was pink, right down to the plush pink carpet upon which sat a full sized white canopy bed. Hello Kitty collectibles cluttered the room. Alex's eyes were overstimulated by all the Hello Kitty things. She hadn't seen anything like this since she was a kid, and maybe hadn't seen anything this extreme even then. *This woman was a serious Hello Kitty collector*, she thought.

The victim was still on the bed. She was covered with a white sheet from the neck down, which meant CSI and the M.E. had already seen her. The arms were exposed, laid out by her sides, but nothing else other than her head could be seen. Manny was about to reach for the white sheet when he heard a familiar voice.

"Detective Castillo, I can save you the visual" Dr. Allison Leavy, the M.E. said as she joined the group. She pushed up thick, black glasses that framed the bridge of her thin nose and stopped next to the bed, looking at Manny with a half smile.

Manny returned Dr. Leavy's smile. She was a transplant from Boston State Police Department and had joined them only two years ago, but she was an extremely intelligent and resourceful M.E. Manny found her to be quick with her autopsies and usually spot on with her assessments. He liked her and more importantly, trusted her.

"Thanks, Allison. I have honestly had enough checking these out lately." Manny chuckled.

Alex looked at Manny then looked at Dr. Leavy. She wasn't sure why but she felt a small stab of jealousy. Alex pinched herself on the inside of her elbow. *Knock it off childish girl,* she chided herself. *It is business and he is your friend- just your friend.*

"...right Alex?" Manny was saying.

They were all looking at her. Alex looked at Manny dazed, pulled from her thoughts, embarrassed at having lost the conversation. She managed an apologetic smile in Manny's direction letting him know she didn't hear what he said to her. He gave her his typical look of concern and turned toward Dr. Leavy.

"Alex hasn't been sleeping much. She has had a lot on her plate lately. Why don't you go ahead and give us a quick break down and then of course we will wait for the final official." Manny said.

"Ok, well the victim was found bound to the bed with these."

Dr. Leavy held up a plastic bag marked with a number for evidence. They held what first appeared to be a wad of pink material, but on further inspection scarves of the Hello Kitty type were what was wadded up in the plastic.

"Her name is Stella Adams. Lividity puts time of death around early Saturday morning anytime after midnight but before four or five a.m. She has ligature marks on both wrists to a lesser degree than we normally see, most likely due to the type of bonding used. She suffered multiple contusions to the face which were perimortem. We know this due to the lack of spreading of the bruises. See how they are smaller and more defined than you might see in someone say who was living and just got out of a bar fight?" Dr. Leavy pointed to the bruises along Stella's face.

"There are definite signs of penetration. She has multiple contusions on the rest of her body as well. We will get her back to the morgue and I will complete the autopsy and send any evidence over the lab. Hopefully get you a hit on CODIS." Dr. Leavy smiled at Alex.

"Dr. Aguilar, how are you doing?" she asked kindly.

Alex looked at Dr. Leavy. This was only the second time they had met. She was surprised at the compassion in her voice. It was palpable. Alex smiled. Any feelings of jealousy she had melted away at that moment.

"I'm okay, Dr. Leavy, thank you for asking." Alex replied.

"I am so sorry to hear of your loss." Dr. Leavy said, genuine concern etched on her face.

"Thank you very much for your kind words, Allison." Alex said.

"Well, I need to get to the morgue." Dr. Leavy announced. "You all have a great rest of your day." Dr. Leavy said her goodbyes and rejoined the CSI team.

Deshawn turned to Manny and Alex and pulled out his little notebook he carried around. He was jittery like a kid at Christmas made to wait too long to open presents. Manny could tell Deshawn believed he was sitting on some good intel.

"I have some of my own information now, Manito." he announced.

Manny smiled and shook his head. Alex had to stifle a giggle. It was not the proper time or place to be laughing but Deshawn had a way of making you want to laugh with some of the things he blurted out.

"Ok shoot!" Manny said.

"Ok so, this lady, Stella Adams…. her boss called in a missing person's report late this morning when she didn't show up for work. He said he knew something was wrong because she hasn't missed a day of work in six years."

"Where did she work?" Alex asked

"It says here that she worked at Connections Cable Company as a dispatcher. She was the one who handed out the schedules and routes to the techs and filled out their time cards," Deshawn said.

"Well, it looks like this could be our guy except there are two things that have me curious. One, this lady isn't a housewife, and two, this time he tied her up. So I can kind of figure that this was probably not consensual this time. But what is the connection between all of the victims?" asked Manny. He was thinking about it when Deshawn cut into his thoughts.

"He also left this, and it is exactly why I was jumping in my pants," Deshawn said. "Hey Marks, can you bring that?" he shouted to one of the CSI guys.

Marks, the guy Deshawn yelled to nodded. A few minutes later Marks came over wearing gloves and carrying a plastic baggie marked with a number. Inside of it was something small, barely noticeable in the dim light. As he got closer they could tell what it was. It was the butt of a smoked cigarette. Deshawn grinned ear to ear.

"I see." Alex said.

"This was my big news," Deshawn smiled.

"Yeah, well, I hate to tell you little buddy, but if the DNA matches from our last vic we still won't have much, remember? He wasn't in the system," Manny said. He sounded disappointed.

"Yeah, I know, but that isn't what I am excited about." Deshawn spoke so quickly Alex almost had to ask him to slow down.

"I am excited because usually to light a cigarette, you have to pick it up, and if you have to pick it up, you have to use your fingers, and if you have to use your fingers you usually leave a…."

"Fingerprint," they all said in unison.

Ah, now Manny realized what Deshawn had been so excited about. Just because the criminal database didn't have a DNA match didn't mean the system wouldn't have a fingerprint match. He smiled wryly at Deshawn.

"You sly little dog, you!"

CHAPTER EIGHTEEN

ALEX AND MANNY HAD JUST FINISHED DINNER WITH Deshawn and his family and were on their way back to Alex's house. The snow had started falling a couple of hours ago, and there was already a few inches blanketing the ground. It was late, and Alex was tired. She was glad tomorrow was Saturday. She thought she might try to sleep in a little bit. Manny had asked her if she needed him to stay the night again. She had told him she thought she would be okay for now. He had assured her that they were still working on her case, and he would certainly let her know if anything came up.

Manny pulled the Mustang into her driveway and killed the engine. Alex didn't want to think about having to shovel the heavy, wet snow tomorrow. Hopefully, they wouldn't get too much and she could let the sun melt it away. Manny looked at her. The moonlight was hitting her face, showering her in its glow. She smiled at him.

"Do you want to come in for a little while? I think I have some Rocky Road ice cream in the freezer." She grinned, knowing all too well that food was too tempting an invitation for him to decline.

"Well, how could I refuse Rocky Road ice cream?" he laughed.

They got out of the car and walked to her front door. The beep of his car alarm echoed as he locked it. Alex gave him a slight roll of the eyes. His eyes widened in apology, and he shrugged his shoulders.

"You know how safe this neighborhood is, and still you insist on locking your car? I don't even lock my windows and, sometimes when I go running, I don't lock the front door either," she announced.

"Well, I can't help it if you are still trusting of this crazy world. I don't know how you could be after what we have seen over the past few years," Manny argued.

"Well, I am able to do my job because I still believe there are good people out there. That is what keeps me going when we see things like we saw today," she retorted.

Manny looked at her, knowing he wasn't going to get very far with her on this subject. Her jaw was set and her brows were pinched together. *Even when she's frowning she's cute*, he thought. He laughed a little.

"Take it easy, Mother Theresa!" he teased. He noticed that she did have to take her keys out and unlock the door. *Good girl*, he thought, you couldn't be too careful in this world. Unlike her, the thought of all the bad people out there was what kept him doing his job. He had taken it on as his personal mission to help rid the world, or at least Massachusetts, of all those assholes.

Alex opened the front door and turned on the hall light. The house was warm and cozy, in immense contrast to the bitter cold outside. She had left the heat on low this morning when Manny picked her up. She heard the weatherman say it was going to snow and be quite cold that evening. Boy, had he been right. It was only about twenty degrees out on the drive home.

Alex threw her purse and keys on the kitchen table. "Make yourself comfy," she said, knowing full well Manny was probably already doing just that. She looked over her shoulder into the living room. Manny had already taken his shoes off and gotten cozy on the couch. She knew Elefantito would be out any minute, more than happy to sit on his lap for a little love. She shook her head, smiling. She kicked off her own shoes, and walked over to the cabinet where the bowls were kept. She pulled two down and rummaged in the silverware drawer for a couple of spoons and the ice cream scoop. She hummed a Dave Matthews song while she got the ice cream ready. *Mmmm, ice cream.* It was one of her favorite foods. She opened the freezer door to take out the ice cream and when she closed it she paused a minute. She thought the door looked a little funny, like something was missing. She stared at it for a minute longer before she realized what was wrong.

"Hey, what is taking so long?" Manny came up behind her just as Alex dropped the ice cream container. It crashed onto the linoleum floor with a thud.

"Hey what the.....?" Many asked surprised by the noise.

Alex turned to look at him, her face drained of all its blood. She looked like she had just seen a ghost.

"Our picture, it's gone," she stammered, pointing to the refrigerator door.

At first, Manny didn't understand what all the fuss was about until he looked at the blank spot where the picture had been taped. They had taken a weekend ski trip together last winter and had such a great time, capturing their fun in three rolls of film. She had taken her favorite pictures of the two of them and hung them on the fridge as soon as they had gotten them back from the one hour photo shop. A piece of lonely tape was still stuck, half on half off, to the empty spot.

"Well, it probably fell off," said Manny, trying to offer her a logical explanation for the missing photo, while halfheartedly looking around at the floor. Alex bent over to pick the ice cream up off the floor, scanning the surrounding area for the photo. It was nowhere to be found. She looked up at him as if to say, "see, it isn't here." Manny thought for a moment.

"Do you think you might have taken it down? Or maybe the cat knocked it off?"

He tried desperately to give her reasons why the picture had gone missing without sounding worried. He didn't think anyone had been in the house or they would have probably noticed it right away. Things would have been moved or messy. Everything looked to be in its place except for the picture. Alex's eyes told him that he needed to come up with a better reason than the ones he was giving her, or she was going to lose it. Then, all of a sudden, he saw a change in her eyes, a realization followed by bewilderment.

"The cat. Why hasn't he come out to greet us?" Alex asked, shakily.

Since she brought Elefantito home, their routine was to always greet each other within a few minutes of Alex coming home. She had been so distracted when they came in that she hadn't really noticed.

Manny thought it was good that Alex had forgotten about the picture for a moment. It would afford him a little time to think about what could have happened to it. He heard her going down the hall, calling to the cat. He looked around the kitchen a little more for the photo. Just then he heard her scream, a blood curdling scream that would have pierced his ears had he been standing next to her. He bolted from the kitchen and raced down the hall into the bathroom where he heard her whimpers.

She stood facing the shower, her eyes wet with tears, her face even whiter that it had been in the kitchen. She kept saying, "No, no, no," as she stood there. Manny was confused.

"What's wrong?" he asked.

He tilted his head up, his eyes following the direction she was staring. That was when he saw it, hanging there by its throat with a pink scarf. Elefantito had been strung up to the shower curtain rod with a winter scarf, his eyes frozen open and his tongue hanging out. Alex fell backwards, and he caught her as she fainted. Manny picked her up and carried her to her bed, laying her down as gently as he could. He couldn't believe it. She hadn't been wrong. Someone had been inside her home. He had to take the cat down and do something with it before she woke up, but he knew he would have to turn this into a crime scene. He pulled his cell phone out of his pants pocket and dialed.

"Hi, this is Detective Castillo. I need a squad car and CSI here." He paused a moment. "A body? No, no coroner. More like animal control." Manny listened as the dispatcher told him they were on the way, and he hung up the phone.

He stood for a moment in disbelief. It had to be the same person who sent the roses. He headed to the bathroom to get a cold washcloth, decided against it, and headed to the kitchen instead. He returned with the cloth just as Alex came to.

"What happened?" she asked, obviously confused.

"You passed out," he said, not wanting to mention the cat to her. He didn't have to, though, because he could see the memory flash across her eyes.

"Oh, god," she moaned.

Alex's eyes rolled back into her head, and she fell back onto her pillow. He thought she might pass out again, but she didn't. She just laid there, tears streaming down her cheeks. He gently placed the cold cloth on her forehead and whispered to her.

"Alex, I know this is probably the last thing you want to hear, but everything is going to be okay." He held the cloth to her head with one hand and placed the other on top of hers. She moaned again but nothing he could understand.

"I have people coming, Alex. They are going to come here, and we're going to figure this out," he tried to assure her. Her body shook as she cried. No sound came from her, but he knew she was listening to him. He tried again.

"We're going to figure this out, Alex. I'm here, and I am not leaving you until we do, okay? But right now, people are on their way. Once they get here, I'm going to drive you to my apartment so you can rest." Manny patted her leg gently.

Alex didn't pull away from his touch, but she didn't respond either. He could feel the sorrow emanating from her body. Then he heard the sirens. The cars flew down her street and into the driveway. Within seconds, it seemed, they were inside the house calling his name.

"In here," Manny yelled.

Two uniformed policemen entered the bedroom, guns drawn.

"Jesus, guys, put those away," Manny yelled.

"Shit, Sir, you scared the hell out of us," Jones said.

Manny knew him. He was a young kid, fresh out of the academy. They were both young, Manny noticed. His partner stood slightly behind him, fumbling with his gun holster. His name tag bore the name "Masterson." He too was probably only a year or so out of the academy.

"Man, when we got the call and then when we saw your car... holy shit! We got nervous, Detective," Jones breathed. His voice cracked as he spoke. Sweat poured down his face even though they were in the dead of winter. Masterson stood quietly behind Jones, but Manny could read the fear on his face. *What the fuck,* Manny thought, *did they have to send me the rookies?* Next time he would make it clear that he wanted *his* people not the fucking newbies. His agitation showed on his face, and both officers shifted around uncomfortably.

"Well, okay then. We have a crime to figure out," Manny finally said, trying not to sound angry.

Jones was first to get moving. Masterson still hung back a little bit, unsure of his next move, and clearly afraid of doing anything wrong in the presence of a superior.

Manny pointed towards the bathroom. "In there," he barked.

Jones headed toward the bathroom while Masterson tentatively took out his notepad. Manny knew the routine. He took a few minutes to explain to Masterson what happened, giving every detail he could think of while looking frequently over at Alex on the bed, checking on her. Masterson listened intently to everything Manny was saying. In the middle of it all, CSI came in and started dusting for fingerprints and taking pictures.

A few minutes later, Deshawn came barreling into the room. Manny looked at his worried face and held a finger up to let him know he would be with him as soon as he could. When Manny was done giving his recount of things, and Masterson had gone to join Jones, Deshawn walked over to him.

"Man, what happened? They called me at the house and told me you had called in to dispatch. I came here as soon as I heard." His face still had lines from his pillow on it, and sleep dust still hugged the inside corners of his eyes. He looked as tired as Manny felt.

"The guys will have to fill you in," he replied. "Right now I have to take Alex and get her out of here. I think she might be in a little shock. She passed out for a while and hasn't said anything since we found the cat. I think I am going to bring her to my apartment. She will be safe there. I am sure whoever did this was the same guy who sent her the flowers. If he could get in here so easily, he might not think twice about coming back a second time," Manny sighed. This was his worst nightmare come true, someone stalking the one person he couldn't live without.

"Okay, sounds like a plan," Deshawn answered. "I will stay here and head up the investigation. You need to try and get some sleep too, Manny. Don't worry about anything right now. I got it all under control. You just go take care of Dr. Aguilar." He patted Manny on the shoulder and smiled reassuringly.

Manny thanked him and walked over to the bed. Alex stirred a little at his touch.

Her legs were cold. He hadn't thought to cover her up with anything in his frantic state. She was still wearing the dress she had on when she had come into the precinct. He walked over to her drawers and was about to grab some clothes for her when he thought better of it. There may be some fingerprints here, and he didn't want to disturb them. He figured he could give her some clothes at his house. They would come back tomorrow, once CSI had finished dusting everything. He returned to the bed and pulled up the afghan that was folded neatly at the end of the bed, wrapping it around her.

He leaned over her and whispered into her ear, "I am going to pick you up now, Alex, and take you to my place. Don't worry, honey. I've got you." Then, gently, he got his hands and arms underneath her and lifted. She was light to him, and he carried her without strain.

"Hey, Masterson, grab my car keys and walk me out the door will you?" Manny ordered.

Masterson did as he was told and followed Manny out of the bedroom. They headed towards the front door. Masterson sprinted ahead of Manny to open the door for him. Manny nodded a thanks to him as he brought Alex outside to the car.

The snow was still falling, and it seemed as if it had picked up a bit. Manny's Mustang was already covered. Masterson unlocked the car for him and opened the passenger side door. As Manny put Alex into the car the afghan slipped off her, falling to the floorboard of the car. Manny bent to pick it up, covered her back up with it, and locked her seat belt into place. He closed the door and watched as her head fell to the side, limp. *She must be sleeping*, he thought. He thanked Masterson and took the keys. When he got into the car he looked at Alex. *Poor Alex,* he thought, *how much could one woman take?* He gently brushed a stray hair away from her face, and his heart ached for her. *I am going to find this bastard,* he thought. No matter what it took, he would do whatever he had to to make sure the son-of-a-bitch paid for what he was doing to her.

CHAPTER NINETEEN

BOBBY WAS LYING ON HIS BED WATCHING THE ELEVEN o'clock nightly news. He was watching the anchor woman with her fake sad face reporting on Stella. When the on-scene reporter outside of Stella's apartment complex came on camera, she looked like her sister had just been killed. Bobby smiled at the thought of Stella and her pretty little Hello Kitty scarf. He wondered if Alex had gone home yet.

Just as he laid his head on his pillow and was about to close his eyes, something familiar flashed across the television screen behind the reporter. He sat straight up in the bed, his eyes glued to the screen. The red Ford Mustang was pulling into the driveway of the apartment complex. Three doors opened almost simultaneously, and he watched as Alex got out of the car with that bastard Castillo and some other guy right behind her. He could see reporters rushing over to them as they walked toward the building. Bobby watched as Castillo grabbed Alex by the arm and ushered her towards the building while the other guy tried to ward the reporters off. Man, he hated that guy Castillo. He was going to do something to him before it was all over. *Yes, something real bad, boy. First, though, you're gonna have some fun with her.*

Alex. Man, she looked good in her dress. It was well fitted and showed her figure. He could see her sleek runner's legs. Her calf muscles were well defined, and she looked much taller than she was with her six inch heels on. He watched as she disappeared into the building.

He sighed when he stood to turn the television off. He stared at the blank screen for a few minutes, trapped in his mind, deep in thought. Then he turned and headed back to the bed.

He stripped his clothes off and lay on the bed stark naked. He reached under his pillow and brought out a small wad of fabric. The panties he had taken from her dresser drawer smelled of laundry soap and a hint of Downy fabric softener. He placed them over his face and closed his eyes. He drew in a deep breath through his nose, inhaling her scent. His body relaxed and images of her danced through his mind. He wondered what she would think when she saw Stella. Would she be sad? Would she be angry? A smile came to his face as he fingered the butt of his Glock 19, touching the safety, as he drifted off to sleep.

CHAPTER TWENTY

ALEX WOKE UP CRYING. DARKNESS SURROUNDED HER. She wasn't exactly sure where she was or how she had gotten there. She went to get up, but a strong hand gently grabbed her shoulder. That was when she saw the outline of Manny sitting next to her.

"Are you okay?" he asked, deeply concerned.

"Yeah, I just had a bad dream," she answered with a raspy voice.

"I heard you crying and came over. I was just about to wake you up when you woke yourself up. Do you need anything?" Manny asked.

"How about a little light?" she asked.

Manny reached over to the bedside lamp, fumbled around a little and found the switch. The studio apartment filled with warm, yellow light with the click of the switch. She knew where she was instantly. It wasn't her first time here.

Manny sat looking at her, waiting for her to speak. She rubbed her eyes for a second, feeling the sting and ache one can only feel after a lot of crying and so little sleep. He looked at her bloodshot eyes and the black circles beneath them. They seemed to have gotten much darker and deeper just overnight.

"Are you okay?" Manny asked again. This time it was more demanding of an answer.

"I don't know. I mean, will I live, yeah. But I feel like I just got run over by a Mac truck," Alex answered, with a little shrug. Manny wished he could help her, make her feel better, take it all away. All he could do was just sit there feeling helpless, unable to do much but listen and be there for her.

"What time is it?" she asked.

"About nine," he answered. She looked at him with groggy eyes.

"I wanted you to be able to sleep," he said.

"Yeah, I guess I needed it. I haven't slept in until nine in a very long time." She smiled.

He could tell it was only a halfhearted smile, but at that moment he would take it. He could also tell she didn't quite understand him.

"Alex, not nine a.m., honey, nine p.m.," Manny said.

Alex looked at him, astonished at what he had just said. She had slept that long? She hadn't slept that many consecutive hours since her parents had died. He let her sit there for a few moments gathering her thoughts.

"I got a call from Deshawn about an hour ago." He stopped, waiting to see if she was going to be strong enough to listen to the rest. She sat for a minute staring at the floor, not looking at him. She took a deep breath in and turned to him.

"What did he have to say?" she asked.

"He said that there were no fingerprints found. He said that they took Elefantito to the veterinary clinic to examine him and that, once they are done, they will release him to you to do what you need to do." Manny looked at her to see if he could continue.

She was sitting up straight, her face expressionless, her breathing calm. *Okay,* he thought, *I guess it is now or never.*

"Alex, I have something to tell you." He sighed heavily then waited. He hadn't wanted to talk about it so soon but he felt she needed to know.

"Okay, shoot," she managed to say.

"Well, when we….. when you found the cat last night, and then I saw him there, um, hanging….." Man, he hadn't wanted to say the words, but he didn't know how else to tell her. He paused for a minute, unsure how to continue.

"Manny, just spit it out." He thought she might jump across the bed and rip the words right out of his mouth if he didn't speak soon. Her face was beginning to flush, a red he had only seen a few times before. He was unsure if she was becoming angry or scared or both, but he knew he had better finish what he had to say.

"Okay, here it goes….. last night after we left and I brought you here, something about the cat was nagging at me, tugging at the back of my brain. So I called Deshawn to tell him not to move the cat. I got you settled in and went back to your house. I watched as they pulled down Elefantito, and that was when I realized what had been nagging me earlier." He paused again.

Alex looked at him, trying to be patient. Her face betrayed her frustration, and he hurried to finish what he was saying.

"The scarf that was around Elefantito's neck was a pink Hello Kitty scarf. It took me a minute to put two and two together, but…" he waited to see if she understood.

Alex squinted her eyes in concentration. Her lips pursed together momentarily while Manny sat, as impatiently as Alex had been only seconds ago, waiting for her to figure it out.

"Don't you see Alex? It was a winter scarf, it was pink, it had Hello Kitty on it…" he prodded.

He watched as her eyes went from cloudy to clear, almost as soon as he had finished his sentence.

"Oh my god, Manny," she whispered, so quietly he almost didn't hear her even though she was only about a foot away from him.

"Now you see," he nearly whispered back. "It is the same guy, Alex. Whoever killed Stella killed Elefantito. He took the scarf from her apartment with the intent to use it on the cat." He talked so fast she could barely keep up with him.

"I also had a hunch that the guy who killed Stella was also our guy who killed the housewives. I had Deshawn put a special rush on the DNA found with Stella to see if it matched the DNA from the housewife. Unfortunately, even ASAP it is going to take about a week to get it back, but…." He paused a moment looking to see if she was keeping up. By the look of horror on her face, he could tell she was keeping up just fine.

"Let me guess," she said. "You're pretty sure the DNA is going to match, right? So our serial killer is stalking me? Is that what you are trying to tell me, Manny?" Alex was on the brink of yelling.

He heard the fear in her voice as it rose to an almost feverish pitch. He looked at her, a deep sinking feeling in his stomach.

"There is some good news, Alex. Deshawn found a link between Stella and the other women. After realizing that Stella had worked for the cable company, Deshawn called her boss again and asked him to fax over the last three months of scheduled appointments for all of the techs. He found all three housewives had been scheduled to have cable installed on the days they were killed. The boss also told Deshawn that all of the women were assigned to a tech named Joe Smith. The boss faxed over a copy of the driver's license. We are hoping that the picture is at least a real one. We know the name is fake, and the address, too. We sent a couple of squad cars over to the address listed on the driver's license but it wound up being an abandoned warehouse. Now we are just waiting to see if we can pull a print off the cigarette." Manny watched her carefully. Her eyes were on him, but he could tell she was reeling with fear.

"Well, at least we have a connection and, hopefully, a face to put to the killer," she finally said, almost sounding a little like herself. She exhaled heavily, shifting around on the bed a little.

"How about some coffee? I could really use some right about now," she smiled.

This time it was a real smile. He smiled back at her, relieved that she had somehow regained her strength.

"I would be more than happy to make you some motor oil," Manny answered.

He got up from the bed and went into the kitchen. Alex stood up on quivering legs, grabbing the nightstand for some balance. She hoped Manny hadn't been paying attention to her. Her stomach flipped with anxiety, and it felt like she had taken shrapnel to the head. She took a few deep breaths and tried to stand again. This time the quivering had lessened, and she was able to stand without the aid of the bedside table.

Alex looked down at her clothes and realized she was no longer wearing the dress she was wearing last night. Instead, she wore an extra large Penn State sweatshirt and a large pair of boxer shorts that had started to slip down her hips. She was relieved to see that she still had on her own bra and panties. Her cheeks flushed in embarrassment. She looked over at Manny and realized he was watching her. He smiled at her, reading her mind.

"Don't worry, Alex. You got yourself undressed last night. Sorry about the ill-fitting, not so fashionable, nighties. But those were the only clothes that I thought might even possibly fit you." He smiled at her sheepishly, and she noticed his cheeks were flushed as well.

"Okay, at least I know you didn't try to take advantage of me in my vulnerable state," she replied, trying to joke her way out of embarrassment. She walked into the kitchen, one hand holding the waistband of the boxers cinched tightly together to prevent any wardrobe malfunctions.

"Well, I am glad that is what you think," he teased.

Alex let out a small laugh as she sat down at the small kitchen table. He put the coffee cup down in front of her. It smelled delicious. On cue, her stomach rumbled protest to the starvation it was being put through. She remembered she hadn't eaten since the night before. Manny must have heard her belly barking orders for food because he chuckled and asked, "Want something to eat?"

"It isn't against the law to want a little bacon and eggs for dinner, is it?" she asked.

"Last time I checked it wasn't," he laughed.

Manny walked over to the refrigerator and started to take out a carton of eggs and a half eaten package of bacon. He pulled out a glass bowl, cracked a couple of eggs into it, and threw the shells into the sink. He put the bacon into the frying pan and turned on the burner. He ran water in the sink, pushed down the egg shells, and turned on the garbage disposal. Alex jumped at the sound it made and spilled some of her coffee onto her lap.

"Ouch, crap!" she yelled.

Manny turned quickly, holding the whisk, stringing egg juice all over the kitchen floor.

"What happened?" he yelped.

"Oh nothing, I just spilled some of my coffee on my thigh and it burned a little, that's all. Nothing I can't handle," she said.

"Well, you scared the bejesus out of me," Manny replied.

There is no doubt that we are both a little jumpy, he thought. He turned back to the stove as she wiped off her legs and the table with a wet paper towel. He hummed a little while he cooked, and she sat quietly, deep in thought.

He finished making their breakfast/dinner, and they sat down to eat together. Alex ate fast, barely tasting the food as it slid down her throat. He could hear her gulping it down. She wasn't worried about acting like a lady around Manny. That was apparent. She had known him too long to start pretending now. He smiled as he watched her. *Man I love her*, he thought. He tried to be strong and seem confident for her, but he couldn't help but feeling scared for her. They had to find the killer before he got to her. He was determined to find him. From that moment on, he made it his only purpose in life...to find the killer. That was when Alex said the words he had been hoping not to hear come out of her mouth.

"Manny, I'm ready to go home now," she said, with her jaw set and her eyebrows pinched. *Oh shit,* Manny thought, *she was serious*.

CHAPTER TWENTY-ONE

"ALEX, YOU CAN'T POSSIBLY THINK IT IS OKAY FOR YOU to go home now," Manny replied.

"Why not?" she asked, as if it were a perfectly reasonable question.

"Well for starters, it isn't safe!" he replied.

If she hadn't known him better, she might have thought he sounded a little condescending. She wiped the thought out of her head. Manny wasn't trying to pick a fight with her, he was trying to talk some sense into her.

"Look, Manny, I am perfectly aware of what is going on. I am aware that it might be a little dangerous for me to go home right now, but that is where I belong. It is where I want to be. I want to sleep in my own bed, fix my own breakfast, and drink my own coffee. Not that I'm ungrateful for all you have done for me, and not that I don't like *your* things, I just want *my* things," Alex said, her eyes pleading with him.

"Well, if I even consider letting you go back to your house, I will be placing a twenty-four hour surveillance on you and your house," he answered, just as indignantly as she had spoken to him.

She wanted to yell at him for saying "if I let you," but she thought again he was only trying to protect her, not control her. Sometimes she was too independent and strong willed for her own good.

"Well, Detective Castillo, you do what you feel you need to, and I will do what I feel I need to. Right now I want a hot bath, a good book, a very large glass of wine, and maybe some more sleep in *my own bed*," she said. Her last few words stung him a little. He knew her well enough to know she wasn't being ungrateful, but still, he'd hoped she would have been more comfortable here with him. He'd hoped she would have been happy to be here with him.

"Okay, Dr. Aguilar, have it your way. But I've got my eyes on you," he laughed. She didn't laugh back.

"Apparently so does someone else," she said, as she stood to clear their plates. She wasn't sure if she was making the right decision to go home. But she knew one thing...she had spent all her life running: running away from friendships, running away from relationships, running away from love, all in the name of fear. *Well*, she thought, *today she was done running*. Starting now she was going to start facing her fears, even if she had to start with the scariest thing so far - a serial killer who, for some reason, had picked her as a target. *Come and get me*, she thought. *We will be waiting.*

CHAPTER TWENTY-TWO

MANNY AND ALEX DIDN'T SAY MUCH ON THE WAY BACK to her house. He had let her borrow another sweatshirt to put over the Penn State one, and a pair of very large sweatpants, to keep her warm. She looked like a small child playing dress up in her father's clothes. It was eleven o'clock at night, and it was only eighteen degrees out. Her nose was still a little red just from walking from the apartment building to the car. He had been so grateful for his electric car starter when they got in and the heat hit them full in the face, warming their frozen cheeks.

Alex watched the cars pass by as they drove, although they were few and far between at this hour of the night. Sunday was a night when most people stayed in, resting up, getting ready to return to work the next day. The sky was clear and she watched as the stars followed them, moving slowly along the darkness. The low hum of the Mustang's engine calmed her. She knew she was doing the right thing. She felt it in her heart. Abuela had always taught her to follow her heart, so tonight she was going to heed Abuela's advice. She smiled as her breath made a spot of condensation on the car window, her breath hot against the cold glass. She reached up and drew a heart for Abuela inside the foggy cloud.

"Hey!" Manny bellowed.

Alex smiled sweetly at him. She knew it would aggravate him, but she couldn't help herself. The car was Manny's "baby." He washed it faithfully every weekend and had the interior cleaned every four to six months. She told him to be careful, that he was going to clean the car to death. Manny didn't think what she said was very funny, but Alex had giggled for some time after.

"What?" she asked, acting surprised.

Alex was trying to lighten the mood a little. She knew Manny was upset with her for deciding to go back home. He had insisted on bringing his things over to stay with her. She agreed to let him stay one night, but after that he would have to go back to his own pad. He didn't like that either, but decided it was better than nothing.

The squad car was already parked out front when they arrived. Manny flashed his headlights to them in greeting, and they flashed their rooftops back in response. Manny pulled into the driveway, just as he had done the night before. *It seems like a million years ago now*, Alex thought. She noticed that someone had been nice enough to shovel her driveway and walkway for her. She smiled, thinking about her elderly neighbors. *It must have been one of Manny's guys*, she figured.

The living room light had been left on. Normally she would be upset with the waste of electricity, but tonight she was grateful to see it on. She opened the car door before Manny had gotten completely around to her side. He reached a hand out for her, and she shooed him away.

"I am not an invalid, my friend," she smiled.

He laughed at her stubbornness. *Typical Alex*, he thought. He held open the door for her as she got out of the car, again holding tight onto the drawstring of the sweatpants she wore. He smiled at her out of character appearance. She looked so small in his extra large clothes. Alex shuffled to the front door in Manny's slippers, one hand holding her pants up, the other holding the plastic bag that contained her clothes from the previous day.

The front door was unlocked and the warmth hit her as she walked in. She stopped for a second, mid step, the memory of last night hitting her hard in the face. She could feel Manny behind her, waiting for her to continue on inside. She walked the rest of the way into the house, hoping that he hadn't noticed her hesitation. He had, of course. Once they were inside, he turned her by the shoulders to face him.

"Alex, I know you very well, and I know how stubborn you can be. If you are unsure about this at all, if you have even the slightest reservations, you don't have to stay here. We can get back in my car and go right back to my place. Please." Manny pleaded with her this time, the argument leaving his voice. She knew he cared about her and that he was only worried about her.

"Manny, I am fine. Really. I want to be home. This is where I live. I am not going to let someone bully me out of my own home," she answered defiantly.

He had known she would give him that kind of answer. He sighed, giving up on trying to get her to change her mind.

"Okay then, I guess it's the couch for me again," he smiled.

Alex returned the favor. They both looked at each other for a moment, locked in each other's gaze. She broke her eyes away first. *It's always the same*, he thought. She was afraid to commit, even leaving her eyes to him for too long was not allowed.

"Well, I am off to the bath. Why don't you turn on the television and see if you can find us an old black and white movie to watch?" Her voice faded away as she walked down the hall towards the bathroom.

CHAPTER TWENTY-THREE

ALEX STOPPED SHORT OF THE BATHROOM DOOR. IT WAS
dark at this end of the house. A little light reached her from the living
room, but not much...just enough to make out where she was going. She
put her hand out timidly, reaching for the light switch on the bathroom
wall. She felt it, cold beneath her fingers. She paused again, unsure if
she wanted to see what was there. She closed her eyes and flipped up
the switch.

The light flickered a few times and was on, humming lowly
as the electrical current flowed through it. Alex slowly opened her
right eye, still keeping the left one squeezed shut, and peaked inside
the bathroom. Everything looked normal to her. No blood, no fur,
no hanging gray tiger cat. She sighed as she blinked twice and fully
opened both eyes. She had known this wasn't going to be easy, but she
never thought it was going to be this hard. She walked slowly over to
the shower and drew back the curtain, holding her breath. She exhaled
when she saw nothing, just her regular old shower and bathtub. She
pushed the shower curtain all the way to the side and flipped up the
lever that plugged the bathtub. She poured in a generous portion of her

favorite lavender bubble bath soap and turned on the water. She turned it as far as it would go to the "hot" side and stripped off Manny's baggy sweatpants, boxers, sweatshirts, and finally, her own panties and bra. She grabbed her brush and combed out her hair. It had been up in a bun since yesterday morning. It felt good to let her hair down, and the brush felt good on her scalp. Just as she was about to get into the bath, there was a light knock on the door.

"Manny?" she asked.

"Yeah, I just thought you might want this," his voice was muffled on the other side of the door.

Alex grabbed her towel and wrapped it around her before she opened the door. Manny was standing there with a smile and a very large glass of Merlot.

"Oh, Manny! You are the best!" she smiled.

"Well, I know my nerves are a little shot, so I know yours must be completely undone. Thought this might help you relax a bit. Nothing like a good bubble bath and a big glass of wine, they say," he grinned.

Alex grinned back at him, grateful for his thoughtfulness. She was glad that he had insisted on coming to stay with her. Even though he was sometimes a stubborn mule, he was a great friend, and he truly cared for her.

"Gracias, mi amigo."

"Okay, well get to it then… commence relaxation mode. Just don't take too long. I don't want to be passed out on the couch when you get out." He laughed as he walked back down the hall.

Alex chuckled at him as she closed the door and returned to her bath. She turned the nozzle to the "cold" setting for a second to let in a little cold water so that she didn't scold the skin right off her body when she got into the tub. When the water was almost spilling over the edge of the bathtub, she turned it off. She used her hand to test the water and mix the cold with the hot. The bubbles floated around, dissipating wherever she put her hand. It smelled wonderful, and her wine tasted great. She dropped her towel to the floor and carefully slid into the tub.

The water was very hot, but it felt good to her aching muscles and tired bones. The bubbles floated around her, popping every few seconds, leaving the smell of lavender in her nose. She laid her head back and closed her eyes. This is exactly what she needed right now. She stayed in the bath for quite a long time, finishing her glass of wine, and getting out only when her fingers started looking like little caramel prunes.

She flipped down the lever and listened as the hole in the tub sucked up the water, burping and guzzling it down into the pipes below the floor. The last of the bubbles lagged behind, hugging the sides of the drain, popping and finally dissipating into thin air. Alex dried herself off, wrapped the towel around her and went into her bedroom. She opened her dresser drawer to get out her nightgown. She decided on the light blue cotton nightgown that came down just below her knees. She slipped it over her head then flipped her head upside down and wrapped the towel around it like a turban. She grabbed her empty wine glass and walked back into the living room.

Manny sat on the couch watching the David Letterman show. Alex couldn't hear much of what he was saying because Manny had the volume down so low. He must not have wanted to disturb her. He had already changed into his shorts and sweatshirt, and his socked feet were placed strategically on the coffee table, comfortably stretched out...but not so that they were in his line of sight. She smiled at how he looked so comfortable, like he was part of the furniture. He must have felt her staring at him because he turned to look at her.

"Hey, girl," he smiled. "How was your tubby?" he asked.

"It was great, but I will tell you that this…" she said, pointing at her empty wine glass, "this was even better." He thought he heard her slur the word "this."

"Would you like another one?" he asked, getting ready to get up.

"Sit, sit. I can serve myself," she insisted.

Manny got comfortable again and watched her pour herself another glass of wine. She filled it almost to the rim. She picked up her glass and walked over to the couch. On her way over she removed the towel from her head and threw it on the back of one of the kitchen chairs. Her hair fell in wet locks all around her face, framing its beauty. Manny sighed.

"No wine for you?" she asked on her way over to the couch.

"Nah, I'm already tired, and that will just knock me out for the count, for sure. I'd rather just chill for a few, and then pass out on this sweet little couch here." he chuckled, patting the couch cushion.

Alex giggled.

"Speaking of that sweet little couch, is there room for me?" she asked.

"You know I will always make room for you, silly." He smiled.

He moved over to the corner of the couch, and she sat slowly, careful not to spill her glass of wine. They sat together for a while, laughing lightly at some of the Letterman jokes. Alex sipped her wine. After Letterman ended, she stood up and yawned.

"Well, I am off to bed," she said. Her eyes were rimmed with red, and a single watery tear fell down her cheek after her yawn. She wiped it and yawned again, laughing.

"Yeah, that sounds like a great idea," Manny replied.

He yawned then, catching Alex's yawning bug. He stood up to get the pillow and blanket off the nearby chair. As he turned to say goodnight, he almost knocked Alex over. She was so close to him he could smell her breath, sweet from the Pinot noir, hot on his face. They stood face to face.

"Manny," she began, then stopped.

"Yes, Alex? Just say it." He could feel some kind of tension between them, like a wire pulled out as far as it could go, ready to snap.

"I...I just wanted to say thank you for everything you have done for me lately. I mean everything. You have really helped me out, and I really do appreciate it. You, I mean. I appreciate you."

She talked a little slower than usual, her words slightly slurred. Alex's eyes were glazed over, and Manny knew she was buzzed.

"I know, Alex. I know you do. Thank you for telling me. It is nice to hear," he said softly.

She reached her hand up and touched his face. Her fingertips sent an electric shock through his body all the way down to his toes. He almost jumped back from it. She must have felt something too because her hand jerked slightly, but she didn't pull it away.

"Can I ...?" her voice trailed off, and she looked away. He watched her struggling with the words inside her head.

"It's okay, Alex. I am not going to bite you," he said, trying to encourage her to speak to him.

Since he had known Alex, it had always been like pulling teeth to get any real feelings out of her. She just closed up when it came to discussing anything like emotions or desires.

"Can I have a hug?" She sounded like a little girl to him.

Without hesitation, Manny leaned over and took her into his arms. She practically disappeared when he fully wrapped his arms around her. *She smells so good*, he thought, his cheek pressed against her head, The clean smell of shampoo and lavender filled his nostrils. Her body trembled slightly. *She must be afraid*, he thought. He held her tighter, trying to soak up some of her fear, trying to take it away from her. She pulled away slightly until her face was close to his. He was so close to her that he could see the flecks of green and hazel swimming in her blue eyes. His body was tingling with excitement. He touched her cheek lightly, cupping her face in his large hand. Her skin was warm. She reached up and held his hand to her face. Manny basked in the moment, taking it all in, committing every feeling, every smell, every touch, to memory. He could feel Alex press her body closer to his. His heart jumped, beating so hard and fast he thought it might explode. He looked into her eyes, big almond shaped eyes, and slowly leaned down. Just then Manny's cell phone rang, and they separated like two teenagers caught in the backseat of a car.

"Oh, um," Alex stumbled.

Her face grew red as she watched him. Manny tried to ignore the phone, tried to recapture the moment, but it was gone as fast as it had come.

"Answer it, Manny," she whispered.

He was about to protest when she turned and left the room. He could tell she was embarrassed. He didn't understand why, but he would have to figure it out later. He looked at the caller i.d. and saw that Deshawn was calling him.

"Yeah, Deshawn, what's up?" he answered, sounding just a tad agitated.

CHAPTER TWENTY-FOUR

ALEX LAY IN HER BED TOUCHING HER LIPS. THEY BURNED as if someone had set fire to them. *Someone almost did set fire to them*, she thought. She listened to Manny talking on his cell phone. She couldn't make out the words, but she could hear the different tones humming as he spoke. Shivers raced up and down her spine. She couldn't believe what had almost happened. Her mind was jumbled, and her hands and feet felt like little ants were crawling all over them. *It is just the wine*, she thought. She should have never had two glasses of wine with Manny around while she was feeling so vulnerable. But how could she have known something like that might happen. She had been drunk around him before and nothing had happened. She tried to make up excuses for herself, for what had almost occurred, but it all sounded so stupid to her at the moment. *There is no real excuse*, she thought, *because it is bound to happen*. She had always liked Manny, no matter how hard she had denied it to him, to Abuela, and, mainly, to herself. She stuffed her feelings down so deep she thought they would never have a chance of surfacing. She was wrong.

Her head was spinning, and her face burned almost as much as her lips. She heard a snap and then Manny quit speaking. He must have finished his phone call and snapped his cell phone shut. She listened for a minute but heard nothing. *He probably went to sleep*, she thought. She knew she wasn't going to be able to sleep, at least for a while. The wine made her tired, but the "almost kiss" had woken her right up. *Ha*, she thought, *Boy, had it*. It had not only woken her up mentally, but physically as well. She had never felt like this before, and part of her really liked the way it felt. The other part of her hated the fact that she had just opened herself up like that. What had she done? She couldn't take it back now. She wasn't sure how she was going to handle it. Maybe she should just pretend it never happened. *Yeah, that will never fly,* she thought. Manny sure wasn't going to "forget it," or act like it had never happened. She had felt the electricity when they were so close, and she knew he must have felt something, too. This was all so new to her, these feelings rushing all over her body. She had never felt this tingling before. She felt it everywhere, like little electrical currents running throughout her body. *Okay*, she talked to herself, *you have to snap out of this right now. You have to go to sleep. Just sleep it off*, she thought. She would have to just deal with it in the morning. There was no way she was going back out there right now to deal with it. She didn't feel safe going out there right now. She wasn't sure what she would do if she did. She wasn't sure if she was in control of herself now. *How much of it was the wine*, she wondered. How much of it was just fate, just meant to be? She shook her head and covered her eyes. *Go to sleep, Alex*. She inhaled deeply a few times to calm herself, but all she could smell was Manny. She closed her eyes and waited for sleep, trying to empty her mind of everything. Eventually, sleep came to her.

CHAPTER TWENTY-FIVE

"I THOUGHT I WOULD LET YOU KNOW THAT WE WERE ABLE to pull a partial fingerprint off the cigarette we found," Deshawn said.

He sounds extremely tired, Manny thought. *Almost as tired as I feel.* Manny stifled a yawn as he tried to concentrate on what Deshawn was saying. He was having a difficult time because right then all he could think about was Alex.

"I had the boys run it through our local CODIS, and they got nothing. So the next step will be to run it through state CODIS. We have to get something," he announced.

Deshawn sounded aggravated. Manny certainly understood. It seemed like somehow this guy was avoiding them each and every way possible. He wasn't sure if it was cleverness or just blind luck, but he was aiming to find out.

"Well, I am sure we will get a hit on either the state or national database. If this guy is killing this often, he has to have a record somewhere else for at least something similar. I doubt he just started killing for the hell of it. Usually, these kinds of killers have a long history," Manny sighed. His body was still tingling.

"Yeah, well we better find something soon. I have a feeling this guy is already on the hunt for another victim," Deshawn said. Manny could hear Muriel talking in the background, and Deshawn covered the phone to answer, his voice muffled.

"Hey, I gotta go now. Muriel has had enough of me being on the phone. Plus, it's late, and we all need our rest," he said, yawning as he finished his sentence. Manny took his cue and followed with a long, deep yawn himself.

"Yeah, buddy, I hear ya. I am a little tired myself. I will talk to you in the morning. I'm going to hunker down on this sofa and sleep like a log," Manny laughed.

"She still got you sleeping on the couch?" Deshawn asked, sounding a little incredulous.

"Yeah, but I am not going to argue. Any gentleman would do the same," he said, poking a little fun at Deshawn.

"Are you saying I'm not a gentleman?" Deshawn asked, sounding hurt.

"Well, let's just put it this way. I doubt you were sleeping on Muriel's couch for very long," Manny said, teasing.

"Well, I've got to hand it to you there, buddy. You're correct in that. I don't even think I spent one night on her couch. I couldn't wait to jump into her bed," Deshawn laughed.

Just as he finished saying that, Manny heard a scuffle in the background and Deshawn saying "ouch." Muriel must have slapped him when she heard his reply. Manny laughed at the thought of her, so much smaller than him, taking him on with a smack to the back of the head.

"Oops, I think I just earned myself a night on the couch, too." Deshawn laughed into the phone, a full hearty laugh that made Manny smile.

"I'd better go before I get another smack. I'll talk to you in the morning." With that, Deshawn hung up.

Manny snapped his phone shut and set the ringer on low. He laid it down on the coffee table and walked over to the bay window to look outside. A light snow had begun to fall and it reflected light from the moon, making the snowflakes sparkle. *We were so close. I could smell her and feel her smooth body. I could feel the electricity coming off her skin,* he thought as he felt a current of excitement flow through his own body. He shivered. Something caught his eye outside, pulling him from his thoughts. The police cruiser sat outside, two uniforms inside. A flicker from a flashlight, two flicks, pause, two flicks. Manny waved to them, assuring them he saw their signal. *Good*, he thought, *they are keeping a watchful eye.* Now he wanted to close his. He walked back over to the couch, laid down, and settled in for the night. The couch was cold at first, but as he lay there it began to warm up, his body heat surrounding him. As he drifted off to sleep, he thought about Alex and how she would act in the morning. Within minutes the only sound in the house was a quiet snore coming from Manny. He had finally fallen into a deep sleep.

CHAPTER TWENTY-SIX

BOBBY SAT IN HIS REGULAR CORNER SEAT AND WAITED. He had been watching Amanda for the last few days now. He needed to shift his attention away from Alex for a while. The cops had been sitting outside her house twenty four hours a day now for what seemed like, to him, a very long time. He assumed that meant they found the cat. Bobby smiled deviously at the thought. He had driven by a few times and noticed the squad car there, every single time. He decided it was best to stay away for now. He didn't want to get caught before he got his hands on the grand prize. He had been so patient, but his patience was starting to wear thin. He wasn't sure how much longer he would have to wait, but knew he couldn't last much longer. It was eating away at him, and the evil was coming more often - asserting itself, getting louder, driving him crazy. He felt his face turning red and forced himself to take a few deep breaths while he hid behind his newspaper. He had been here all morning, just like he had for the last few days. Normally, he would leave after Alex came in. But she hadn't been in for a while.

Amanda was scheduled to get off work soon. She bustled around...cleaning, taking orders and filling them. *She has a decent smile*, he thought. He wondered if she could feel him watching her because every so often she would look at him. He would smile at her sometimes, and other times he would look away quickly so that she didn't think he was staring at her. She smiled back a few times. He didn't know if she was just being nice or if she liked him. He hoped it was the latter. He was starting to think about her more than he had ever thought of her before. He thought that maybe today he would have the nerve to talk to her.

Bobby almost missed her saying goodbye to the manager. She grabbed her purse and keys and headed out the front door. He quickly grabbed his stuff and headed out after her. He didn't think she had a car, so he followed behind her for a minute, not wanting to scare her. Just as he came up behind her, she stopped walking and turned around abruptly.

"Can I help you?" she asked. She didn't look surprised that he was behind her.

"Um, hi," he managed to get out of his mouth. Bobby nearly stutter-stepped back when she spoke to him. She had caught him off guard when she had stopped, and it took him a second to gather himself.

"Hi," she said offering a partial smile.

He could tell she was a little unsure if she should be talking to him or not. He smiled back at her, trying to make her more comfortable, trying to make her see he meant her no harm. *At least not yet,* he thought. His smile grew bigger, and he had to stifle a laugh that threatened to escape his mouth.

"I'm Jake. I hope you don't think this too forward of me, but I have been seeing you every morning for the past, I don't know, long time anyways, and I…." he trailed off, waiting for her to invite him to finish. This time a full smile graced her lips.

"Yeah, I noticed you looking at me. I was almost starting to wonder if you were some kind of creep or something. You're lucky I didn't call the cops." She laughed at her own joke, and he had to force a laugh so that she couldn't tell that what she said made him uncomfortable, and even a little angry. *How ironic*, he thought, *I would have been in deep shit if she had called the cops.*

"No, I'm not a creep. I just know a beautiful woman when I see one." He paused, trying to look embarrassed, his face turning a little red. "Oh, I hope that wasn't too much for you." He managed a nervous laugh and a shy smile.

He wasn't quite sure how this was going to go. He had never had to try and prove himself with the others. He had already been in a situation where he knew he was in control. All he had to do was wait for the others to throw themselves at him. This was the first time that he was going to have to make the first move. This was a new experience for him, and it excited him.

She blushed slightly at his advances, but she kept smiling. She hadn't run away yet, so he figured he was doing alright so far. She turned away for a minute, and his stomach flipped. *Oh no*, he thought, *maybe I overestimated my charm*. His fears were squelched quickly when she turned back to him and said, "No, it wasn't too much."

"I don't know what you like to do," he continued, "but I just bought an ounce of weed, and I was wondering if you might like to partake with me?" he snickered.

He hadn't been sure if this would be the right approach, but she seemed to be the kind of girl who might dabble in a little extracurricular activity now and then. He knew he was taking a gamble that she might just run away and tell someone, especially if she wound up being a real straight-laced kind of girl.

A smile spread across her face, this time wide and real. He guessed he had hit a chord somehow, because now he could tell he had her full attention. She looked around for a second, surveying her surroundings, thinking about something. He let her stand in silence for a moment. He didn't want to interrupt what she was about to say.

"How did you know?" she asked quietly, looking around as if she were being followed.

"Oh, I didn't. I was just hoping." He smiled at her, warm and inviting.

He had worn all black clothes today and had spiked up his blonde hair a little bit, trying to look as Goth as possible. He thought by how she dressed that it might attract her to him a little more than if he had worn a suit and tie. He had spent some time just observing her so that he could get this right.

"Well, I live just down the street. Maybe you could come over, and we could smoke there and hang out for a while," she said, her eyes looking at him, then looking away, then looking back at him. He figured she had done this before, but he could tell that it still made her a little nervous. He smiled at her again, trying to put her at ease.

"Okay, if that is okay with you," he said, feigning concern.

"I wouldn't have asked you over if it wasn't," she replied.

Her trepidation seemed to dissipate into thin air. Amanda grew more confident as the seconds passed and, the next time she spoke, her tone reflected it.

"Well, let's get going," she said, "before we freeze to death out here."

CHAPTER TWENTY-SEVEN

ALEX WOKE TO THE SOUND OF BIRDS WHISTLING SING-song notes outside her bedroom window. She pulled the covers up over her face. It was freezing in her room. She had forgotten to close the bedroom window last night in her drunken state of mind. *No*, she thought, *it wasn't because you were drunk. It was because of the near kiss.* It had thrown her all out of whack. She smiled a little under the armor of her covers. The blankets felt warm, enveloping her in a safe, dark cocoon. She knew she would have to get up at some point and face Manny, but she wasn't sure if she was quite ready to do just that. She lay there, in darkness, reliving last night's events. As she thought about it all over again, her lips began to tingle with the rest of her body, longing to complete the unfinished kiss. She quickly banished the thoughts and whipped the covers off her body. She shivered against the cold. Alex walked over to her bedroom window and shut it with some defiance. She was not going to let a little "almost" kiss ruin her friendship with Manny.

She put on her fuzzy blue slippers and shuffled down the hall-way into the living room. Manny was already up, talking quietly on his cell phone. He looked up as she came into the living room and smiled at her. *Good old Manny*, she thought, *hopefully, he was going to pretend nothing happened, and that will suit me just fine.* She listened as he spoke.

"Yeah, okay. Great! That is great news, Deshawn. I will see what Alex has planned for the day and, hopefully, we can both swing by. Okay, yep, okay, see you in a bit." He finished up with a goodbye and shut his cell phone with a smile.

"Well?" she asked, knowing something was up by the triumphant smile displayed on his face.

"Well, Deshawn says we got a hit off the national criminal database from the partial print we got off the cigarette. Also we got the fax from the boss over at Connections Cable Company. It is a picture of the person we are hoping is our guy. Deshawn says it's a little blurry, but that we will be able to get a little look at this guy," Manny said, looking happy.

"Well, that's big news," Alex said. She was hoping with every cell of her body that Manny wouldn't mention last night.

"So, do you have any plans? Do you have any patients lined up for today, or do you think you can take a ride with me downtown to check out our man?" he asked, looking hopeful. She thought for a moment.

"I actually don't have anyone lined up until two this afternoon, so I don't see that it would be a problem to take a ride with you." Alex smiled, then tried to wipe it off quickly, not wanting to give Manny any reason to remember last night. She hoped what she had said hadn't sounded misleading.

"Okay. Well, if you don't mind, I think I will jump in the shower and get ready. Then when you are ready we will head to the precinct." Manny turned to walk towards the bathroom.

Alex let out a sigh of relief as she watched him start to walk away, thinking that he wasn't going to say anything about last night. When he stopped and turned to look at her, her breath caught in her throat.

"By the way, Alex," he smiled "I would have really liked to have felt your lips last night. I think it would have been amazing."

With another brilliant smile, Manny turned and walked away. *Damn him*, she thought, even though she couldn't suppress the smile that came to her lips this time. *Yeah*, she thought, *that is one I can't argue with Detective.*

CHAPTER TWENTY-EIGHT

MANNY LED THE WAY UP THE TWO FLIGHTS OF STAIRS TO his office. Uniformed police men and women filled nearly every space available. Some walked up and down the stairs, some were off to the side talking, some stood around reading what might have been notes, and others sat at desks typing or answering phones. They reminded Alex of worker bees buzzing around the nest making honey...buzz, buzz, buzz. She smiled a little at the thought. Manny looked back at her to make sure she was keeping up.

"What's so funny?" he asked, seeing the smile on her face.

"Nothing. I was just thinking of something, that's all," she answered.

She could feel her face getting red as blood flowed to it with embarrassment. It would be awful if any of the cops thought she was making fun of them. She looked down at the stairs to check her footing, but mainly to avert her eyes from Manny's. It seemed like he could always tell what she was thinking.

"Okay, but I know that look," he answered, as if he had just heard her thoughts. *Damn him*, she thought again. How could someone know her so well? It almost drove her nuts sometimes. But sometimes it brought great solace to her, knowing that she didn't have to say anything. When she was feeling bad or down, he just seemed to know, and always tried to console her.

Manny reached the door to the Homicide Unit. Alex thought it was very similar to her door at work. The same kind of frosted glass with black letters printed neatly on the front. She thought about work and how much time she had taken off recently. She hoped that it wasn't affecting her patients too adversely. Lola had made a point to tell her that she needed to take care of herself first before she could properly take care of anyone else. *Oh, Lola*, Alex thought, *what would I do without you?*

"Hey, you two!" Deshawn almost yelled from across the room.

Alex could tell by his voice that he was pumped up. She figured it was because of the recent leads. He smiled his big, beautiful smile at them as they worked their way through the maze of chairs and desks toward him.

"Hey, yourself," Manny answered back.

She loved the way they were together, kind of like she and Manny were together. *Stop it, Alex*, she thought, pushing the very words out of her head.

"Come on over. I have some things to show you." Deshawn waved them over to two chairs that he had strategically placed around the computer screen. He sat back down in the "captain's chair" that was right in front of the screen and started punching on the keyboard. Alex listened to the clicking sound for a few minutes, thinking that Deshawn was actually quite a good typist. There weren't too many pauses between clicks, and he used both hands to type...not like Manny, who used the index finger method, slow and methodical. She smiled and thought that if Lola ever quit on her she could hire Deshawn to take over. She could imagine him being quite good at typing her case notes.

Within minutes, a picture of a young man appeared on the screen. It was a mugshot of a teenager, sad-faced. He was blonde with freckles splayed out across his nose and cheeks, but his eyes were what caught Alex's attention. They were set deep into his face...dark, black, almost empty eyes. Her stomach flipped a little at the sight of him. She didn't recognize him, but she thought that he might be someone who could definitely hurt someone. His eyes said it all.

"Says here that this young man is Robert Benson, Jr., called Bobby by all that knew him. He was just fifteen when this picture was taken. He was locked up in juvenile detention until the age of twenty for killing his then girlfriend, Angela Stewart, and their unborn child." Deshawn read the report that appeared underneath the picture. Alex sighed at the information, thinking that the eyes never lie.

"The partial fingerprint we got off the cigarette matches this Bobby Benson, Jr. When I dug deeper for more information on him, I found out that his father, Robert Benson, Sr., is serving life without parole for the murder of his wife, Lillian Benson, when little Bobby was only seven years old. That could really fuck you up, I guess," Deshawn said with a cynical kind of laugh.

"Oh, man! Sorry, Dr. Aguilar." He caught himself.

Alex smiled at him, knowing the routine. Deshawn always tried really hard to be respectful of her when she was around, but she had actually been thinking along the same lines.

"No apologies please, Deshawn. I was actually going to say the same thing myself." She smiled a sad smile at him.

Manny watched her, knowing that her psychologist side was working. *Same sweet Alex, always feeling sad for the predator if she sees them as a victim.* He hoped that the last bit of information wouldn't skew her realization that this man was very dangerous. Even if he had watched his mother being brutally killed by his father, it didn't make him any less dangerous. Alex caught Manny looking at her and knew instantly what he was thinking.

"I know, Manny, I know. But you have to at least feel a little bit sorry for him," she answered.

"No. No, I don't. A lot of people have seen one parent killed by the other parent, and it doesn't send them on a lifelong killing spree, Alex. One of these days you are just going to have to face it, Alex. Some people are just born bad," Manny replied.

Alex looked away from him and back to the computer screen. Deshawn waited for them to finish. It hadn't been the first time he had listened to this argument. It seemed like the only thing Alex and Manny ever disagreed on was whether people were inherently evil. Deshawn leaned more towards Manny's theory. He and Manny had seen too much bad shit to feel otherwise. He leaned over to the printer and pulled a piece of paper from it, handing it to Alex.

"Do you recognize this man, Dr. Aguilar?" he asked.

Alex held the piece of paper in her hand. It was a picture of a driver's license issued in the state of Texas. An older version of the young man on the computer screen stared at her from the driver's license photo. His eyes sent shivers down her spine. *It is definitely the same person*, she thought.

"Hey, wait. I think I have seen this guy before, but for the life of me I cannot place him. I'm not sure where I have seen him, but I know I have," she said, not moving her stare from the picture. The cold black eyes glared at her, holding her there.

"Well," Manny said, "then I am quite sure this must be our guy. If he isn't our guy, he at least knows something regarding our cases, and so that makes him a prime suspect. I want an APB put out on this guy, and I want him in the interrogation room A.S.A.P." Manny gently took the paper from Alex's hand and gave it back to Deshawn.

"We won't go to the media yet. We will put out the APB and hope we can find this guy while keeping it as quiet as possible for now. We should exhaust all our leads before we let those bloodhounds get hold of it." Manny put his hand on Alex's shoulder. "I know that you will remember where you have seen him if you just have a little rest and think about it a little, Alex. As soon as you remember, you let us know. Deshawn, I am going to take Alex to work, and then I'll be back. She has a couple of patients this afternoon, and we only brought my car in."

Manny turned to Alex and put his arm around her. He felt her shudder a little and knew she was afraid. He wished he could take it all away for her. *Soon,* he thought, *soon I will have that son-of-a-bitch in my grasp.*

CHAPTER TWENTY-NINE

THE NIGHT WAS FREEZING, AND SNOW AND ICE HAD FALLEN for the last five hours. The sound of the doorbell woke her from a deep sleep. She lay there for a moment, listening to the mumble of voices coming from the living room. She grabbed her stuffed elephant and walked quietly into the living room. Abuela was sitting on the couch, hunched over, tears streaming down her face. Two policemen stood watching her saying how sorry they were for her loss. Alex looked at Abuela again. Why was she crying? Abuela looked up just then, feeling her presence, and wiped her face hurriedly.

"Hola, mija. What are you doing awake?" she asked.

"I heard the doorbell, it woke me up." Alex's voice was so small, so young. "Vente. Come sit next to me. We will talk for a while," Abuela said.

Abuela looked up at the policemen, told them thank you, and walked them to the door. After they had gone, she went to the kitchen to make Alex some hot chocolate. Alex watched her work, Abuela keeping her back towards her the whole time. Alex knew something was wrong. Abuela wasn't the kind of woman who cried very often. Alex looked outside the bay window and watched as the snow fell quickly and heavily. The snowflakes were very large, visible only by the glow of the streetlamp. The sky was black, and Alex imagined that there were some large dark clouds hovering above, crying drops of water that froze before hitting the ground. Abuela returned to the living room with the hot chocolate and sat beside Alex on the couch. Alex watched as the tiny marshmallows melted slowly in the pool of hot brown liquid. Steam rose past the white puffs of sugary balls, dancing into the air before disappearing. Alex waited in silence, knowing that Abuela was about to tell her something very important, wondering when she would finally speak. Alex looked up at her when she heard her sigh. Tears were once again falling from Abuela's eyes.

"Mija, I have something very important to tell you, and I want you to listen very carefully." Abuela shifted uncomfortably on the couch. "Your mama and papa went to Heaven, Cielo, tonight to see Jesus. Their spirits have gone to God. Even though they are not here in body, they will be watching over you from Cielo until you are able to join them," Abuela said.

"Why did they go tonight?" Alex asked, as big crocodile tears dropped from her chin onto her nightgown.

"Well, mija, it was just their time. They had spent enough time here, and it was time for them to go to God to spend time with him," she answered.

Alex wasn't quite sure if she believed in the "Cielo." She struggled with the idea, especially now when it had to do with her own parents. Alex again stared at her hot chocolate, wondering when it would cool. As she watched it, she was suddenly gripped with fear. She didn't want to look up from her warm cup of cocoa, afraid of what she might see. The tiny hairs on the back of her neck stood at attention, and goose bumps began to rise all over her quickly cooling skin.

When she looked up, Abuela was gone. She was all alone, yet she was not. She looked around, and her eyes caught the shadow and stayed there, unable to turn away. A tall, hulking silhouette loomed in the bay window, watching her, waiting for her. She sat frozen by the fear that pulsed through her body. Her blood turned to ice, and her body turned to stone. She was paralyzed, unable to move. That was when she heard it, far away at first, as if it were coming from the deepest depths of an empty cavern. It grew louder and louder, coming closer, until the sound was booming throughout her head. A banshee, screaming with fear and rage...

"Run, mija, run," Abuela screamed at her, her voice resonating through her soul. As if released from some stranglehold, Alex stood and began to run. As she ran the living room faded away from her, and she was in a dark tunnel, a small sliver of light ahead of her.

"Run, mija, run!! Faster... " Abuela continued to scream at her.

Alex's heart pounded in her chest, threatening to explode through the skin that held it there. She knew if she lifted her shirt then, she would actually see the outline of her heart as it tried desperately to escape her chest cavity. The shadow followed close behind her. She could almost feel the heat from its breath on the back of her neck. Alex ran and ran, not knowing how fast she was going, not knowing how far. As she ran, though, the slit of light that called to her never grew any bigger, never opened up to welcome her. Her feet grew slower and slower. Why? What was holding her back? The shadow grew closer, and she could almost taste its breath. She could smell its sweat and hear its huffing breath. It was almost upon her. She tried to will her feet to go faster. Just then she looked down to see what was keeping her there. She saw the thick liquid, enveloping her feet every time she stepped. It was dark and viscous. What is it? Her mind raced, trying to force her feet to move, but she realized she was running in place...

not moving forward, not moving anywhere, just running, static, stuck in the thick puddle of........ blood. With the sudden realization that her captor was upon her, terror ripped through her body, and she let loose a blood curdling scream. She was running in blood, and she wasn't going anywhere. It held her there like flypaper, covering her feet and legs. But where is it coming from? She quickly assessed herself as the shadow came upon her. It was her blood, flowing like thick, muddy water that had broken through a dam. The front of her nightgown was covered with it, just below her waist, gushing from between her thighs. Oh god, she whispered as the shadow enveloped her, pulling her down into the darkness. She managed to let out one last scream as it overtook her....

Alex woke screaming. Her voice echoed through the empty house, and the sweat poured from her body. Her heart was pounding in her chest as if she had really been running. She shook all over, her breath coming in small spurts, hurting her throat as it forced itself in and out, in and out. She sat for a moment, still feeling like she was under the spell of the dream. Alex reached over, clumsily turning on the bedside lamp on the third try. Her nightgown was drenched, and she saw the pool of sweat that surrounded her, a dark outline encircling her on the bed sheets. She looked over at the alarm clock. It read three a.m. She stood and walked over to her dresser. She opened a drawer and reached in for a new nightgown. She pulled the wet gown over her head and threw it into the dirty clothes hamper. She put the dry nightgown on and pulled her damp hair up into a bun.

Alex walked back over to the bed and covered over the wet spot with the comforter. She lay back down and used the afghan that Abuela had made her to stay warm. Alex wanted to close her eyes, but they stayed open. She was afraid of the picture they might show her if she willed them shut. The memory of the dream kept trying to rear its ugly head and, each time it tried to suck her in, she willed it out of her mind. She hadn't been sleeping very well lately. This was the first night Manny hadn't stayed over. She had told him to go home after almost a week of camping out in her living room, and he had finally given in and left. Now, she was wishing he was here. She could use someone to talk to, to take her mind somewhere else for a little while.

It had been a few days since they had found out the information about Bobby Benson, Jr., and no other leads had come up since. Manny tried to get her to stay with him until they found their suspect, but Alex insisted that she belonged at home. She lay in bed for another hour, unable to sleep. She thought about this Bobby Benson, Jr. She wondered what kind of life he had growing up before he witnessed his mother's murder. She figured it was most likely a life of physical and mental abuse, and possibly even some sexual assaults by his father. It hadn't said anything about sexual abuse being evident in any of his psychological profiles. He had seen at least a dozen psychiatrists and psychologists. The last one had actually prescribed him Lorazepam, and she wondered if it worked for him at all. She didn't know for sure, because a week after his last entry on Benson, the psychiatrist had come up missing. Law enforcement had found his body three weeks later, bloated and barely recognizable, in the local river of the town he had lived in since he was born. Alex figured Bobby Benson had probably had a hand in that drowning, as did the police from that little town. They had issued a warrant for Bobby Benson, Jr.'s, arrest. Of course, he was never caught. She assumed that he immediately fled. She wondered why he had killed the psychiatrist. Had he gotten too close? Had he gotten too deep into Benson's mind? She thought he probably had. She wondered what it would be like to talk to this man. Would be so sick that he wouldn't make much sense, or would he be intelligent and articulate, even charming. She tossed it over in her mind for a few minutes, sighing heavily.

Alex decided to get up and take a run. That would help clear her mind. It was still dark outside. They were deep into the winter months now, and it wasn't light until around six a.m. She got dressed and bundled up. When she went to sleep it had been snowing, and she hoped they had plowed a little. If not, she would be in for a tough run. At that point, she didn't care how hard it was going to be. She just needed to get out of the house for a while. She threw the scarf around her neck, put the skull cap over her ponytail, pulling it down over her ears, and opened the front door with her mittened hand. She looked around for a split second, remembering the shadow that had been lurking in her dreams. She longed for the squad car that had been permanently parked in front of her house for six days. It left a few days ago. Manny told her that his chief said they couldn't afford to keep surveillance on her anymore, with all the crime happening lately and the unsolved murders that were still under investigation. There was no reason to keep them there, especially since nothing else had happened following the cat incident. She forced a little laugh from her lips, scolding herself for being so scared.

Alex inspected the neighborhood. There was about three inches of new white snow on the ground. She bent over and scooped up a little into her hand. It melted fast in the warmth of her knitted palm. She was grateful that it was the lightweight, powdery stuff that was easy to shovel. Her hand began to freeze even through the mittens, and she flung the remaining snow onto the ground. She rubbed her hands together to warm them up and headed down her driveway towards the sidewalk, each step coming faster and faster until she worked herself up to running stride. She smiled, relieved to be out of the house...relieved to be away from the dream. As she ran, she inhaled the cold air deep into her lungs and let it out in a cloud of white vapor. She knew by the time she was done with her run, she would be completely away from the whole experience, and she couldn't wait.

CHAPTER THIRTY

BOBBY YAWNED DEEPLY AND WATCHED AMANDA AS SHE slept. He had been in her apartment with her since early afternoon. The clock on her cable box read three a.m., and he was growing tired. They had smoked the weed he had brought, and then polished off two bottles of wine. Amanda had passed out a few hours ago. He smiled as a small snort came from her. He looked around her apartment. It was very small. She didn't have much, but it was quite cozy. She lay on the couch, one arm under her head hung halfway off the torn cushion, the rest of her body curled up in the fetal position. *She looks comfortable*, he thought, *deep in the world of drunken sleep*. The small tattered coffee table looked like it was purchased at a yard sale or the Salvation Army. Chunks of wood were missing, leaving yellowish misshapen spots here and there. It was cluttered with wine glasses, pot seeds, unused wrapping papers, and a pile of ash from the incense burner. Half of it spilled over the holder and onto the table. Another incense stick burned almost to its end, the smoke curling up into the air, the ash falling to land on the pile that had formed. He thought if he had super-human hearing he would hear it thud as it hit.

Bobby lit a cigarette and inhaled deeply, enjoying the way the smoke burned his throat and lungs. He exhaled, blowing the smoke towards the smoke of the incense, watching as the plume from the incense and the puff of smoke from his mouth fought for the same space of air. His eyes returned to Amanda. He stared at her while he smoked. He had spent the whole afternoon and evening with her. She was quite an intelligent woman. They spent most of their time together discussing politics, music, her past, and her future.

She had gone to UMASS Lowell for a while to study business and financial planning, but had fallen on hard times when her boyfriend of two years suddenly broke it off with her. She told Bobby how deeply depressed she had become. How she had stopped eating and dropped down to 98 pounds. At the end of four months, she tried to kill herself. She sheepishly removed her watch and bracelets to reveal the scars on the insides of her wrists.

Bobby didn't want to, but he found himself feeling a little sad for her, remembering the pain and anguish he went through when his first love broke it off with him so suddenly. He felt a sort of kinship with Amanda. Bobby held her arm out and gently traced the scars with his fingertips, almost like his mother used to trace the scar on his face with her fingers. Amanda had blushed a little when he touched her, but she hadn't pulled her hand away. She allowed him to continue to touch her. He considered kissing her then, but didn't. When he decided not to kiss her, he dropped her hand suddenly. She seemed a little confused, pulling her arm into her stomach, folding both arms around each other and herself protectively. She never said anything, but he knew at that moment he made her a little uncomfortable. He smiled at her and poured them each another glass of wine. She smiled back and took one, forgetting how strange she felt for that split second. They drank and talked for the next three hours, until she finally laid her head down on the couch and fell asleep. There had been a few different times throughout the night where he could have taken her, but he hadn't. He wasn't sure now, watching her sleep, why he hadn't. But he thought now might be a good time.

He stood up and walked into the meager kitchenette. It was very small, and there were no table and chairs, just a small counter top, a few cabinets, and a small refrigerator. An old oven, whose top appeared to have never been cleaned by the looks of the food crusted all around the burners, sat next to a small sink containing a few dishes piled in it. Food was caked on some of them as well. He watched as a fly hovered above a cereal bowl that was still full of a milk and water combination, a corn flake stuck to its rim. He could hear the buzzing sound as the fly decided where it was going to land. Bobby hated the noise it made and wanted to smash it with his hand. He took his lighter and lit it a few times near the fly. The fly, as stupid as it was, never moved far from the dishes, unable to determine that the danger of returning was far greater than the pleasure of the food it was trying to get. As the fly swooped in again, Bobby waited patiently until it was close enough. With the lighter already burning in his hand, he placed the flame to the fly. He watched as its wings began to melt and its body twitched and writhed inside the flame. It only took a few seconds. He left the burnt fly in the kitchen sink and walked over to the counter, where he had spotted a set of kitchen knives earlier on in the evening.

He removed a few knives, one by one, and inspected them. They were shiny, with nice thick, heavy handles. This was one thing that it seemed she had actually spent a little extra money on. *Probably a gift*, he thought. He pulled one out, replaced it back into its wooden slot, pulled out another, decided it was too small and replaced it. On the fourth try Bobby found the one he liked. It was a large carving knife with a twelve inch blade, a very sharp point, and a sharp, beveled edge.

He turned the knife on its side and smiled at his warped image shining back at him from its smooth blade. He played with the knife for a few minutes before he took the tip and dug it slightly into the thick pad of his left index finger. A spot of blood came almost instantly to the surface, spreading out between the skin and blade tip. He removed it from his finger and looked at the small drop of blood. It was dark red and moved slowly as he turned his finger from side to side. Just before the drop spilled from his finger to the floor he caught it in his mouth, sucking in a little. He waited until there was no more blood coming from the skin to remove his finger from his mouth. He looked at the skin that he had sucked on, wondering how it got so puckered. *It looks like a raisin or prune*, he thought. He grabbed the dish soap and washed the knife with soap and hot water, then dried it with a paper towel, putting the used paper in his jeans pocket.

He walked over to the couch where Amanda slept and looked down at her for a few minutes, considering what he might do. She must have felt him looking at her even in her sleep because, for the first time since she had passed out, she stirred a little. She muttered something under her breath and turned onto her back. He smiled at this, thinking how great it was that she had just rolled over and exposed herself to him. He went over and gently lifted her off the couch and onto the bean bag that lay next to the couch. She moved around again, whispering something. He could smell her breath, a nice mix of pot and wine, and he wondered what her lips were going to taste like. He straddled her and opened her sweater up, displaying a tight t-shirt that read "Down with Bush" with a peace sign stamped right between her breasts. He lifted the bottom of the thin t-shirt and placed the carving knife to it. He held the shirt taut and rubbed the knife gently upwards. It didn't take much, the knife was very sharp, and the shirt material was so thin that it cut almost like butter. It made a slight ripping sound as the knife traveled easily up to her neck. It stuck there for a moment, the collar on the t-shirt a bit thicker than the rest of the fabric. He pulled a little harder on the end of the t-shirt and made a slight jerking motion with the knife. It ripped through the collar, and Amanda moved under the motion. He lifted the strap of her bra that lay between her breasts and placed the knife, flat side down, against her skin. The cool metal woke her from her sleep with a start. Her eyes were blurred with confusion. Had she been sober, he thought, she might have started fighting him off from the start. But instead, a lazy smile spread her lips.

"Hey, there," she said, still smiling up at him.

He thought she had been making advances at him all night, but he had thwarted them. She grinned in recognition, a coy smile, a knowing smile. He felt her move slightly beneath him.

"So, you don't like the bra, huh?" she asked.

She grabbed his hand that held the knife and helped him turn the sharp side upwards until the blade caught the material of her bra. He smiled and yanked upward again, slicing through the strap. He moved his free hand over each half of the bra removing the cups from their spots, exposing her breasts. They fell free of the restraints, full and large, her nipples erect in the slight cold. She giggled a little. He moved above her, one hand cupping her breast, the other moving the blade of the knife gently over her stomach. Her pale flesh dimpled a little under the light pressure. He wasn't sure how she was going to take having a knife on her, but either way he didn't care. It was arousing him, and that was all that mattered. She didn't seem to mind the knife as he took her nipple into his mouth, letting his tongue tickle it lightly, then sucking it in almost painfully. She gasped and moaned a little under the pressure. He felt her hands on his back, her nails digging into his flesh through his shirt a little as he sucked on her other nipple. She had on a skirt, and he felt her spread her legs a little. He let his tongue wander down to her navel, licking, tickling, dancing around. When he made it to the belt of her skirt, he stopped and looked up at her face. Her eyes were closed and her breath came a little quicker than before.

He sat up, positioning himself between her legs. He brought the knife to the bottom of her skirt, again holding the material taut in his free hand and the knife facing upwards, hugging the material, ready to cut.

"Yes," she moaned, and he cut, slightly off center away from the zipper and button.

The knife worked a little harder on the skirt material, but still cut nicely, cleanly. Her skirt fell limp to the floor behind her, giving him the full view of her body. She was only wearing a thin pair of bikini panties now, and he felt the familiar tingle in his groin. He pushed his pelvis up against her and she moaned, feeling the hard bulge in his pants. Her lips parted in another gasp, and she reached to undo his pants. He helped her pull himself out of his pants. He ripped his shirt off and threw it on the couch. She looked up at his muscular body, his skin firm over the muscles, his veins popping everywhere, the blood coursing through his body. He crouched over her naked, and she saw he was very large, fully erect. She watched the veins pop out on his manhood, and she beckoned him over to her. She reached down to pull off her panties, and he stopped her, motioning to the knife. She smiled again, nodding in agreement. He slit each side of her panties and peeled them off of her. She giggled again in delight. He paused, watching her. She moaned and reached down for him, grabbing him gently and guiding him into her. He entered her and a deep shudder of pleasure erupted from him as he realized how wet and warm she already was. She took him in, and he moaned. He was surprised to realize she could take all of him. No other woman had been able to fully accept him before. This excited him beyond anything, and he moaned in pleasure. She moaned with him, and they moved together for a while, in rhythm to a beat only they could hear.

"Oh, my God, you are huge," she giggled.

He laughed a little. She groaned a bit as he pushed a bit harder, a bit deeper. Still, she took him in...all of him.

"Faster," she begged, as she began to climax. He did what she said, moving faster and going as deep as he could, feeling her hugging him, her skin moist, kissing him there. "Oh, God," she moaned.

He moved faster still, bringing himself to an almost feverish pitch, and she cried out underneath him, not in pain, but in pleasure. Again, he was surprised. He moved his hands all over her body, and as he moved his fingers over her mouth, she grabbed them and put one in her mouth, licking it, biting it, sucking on it. He liked her, he couldn't help himself. She bit his finger a little harder, and he smiled. That was when she surprised him the most, grabbing his hands and placing them around her neck. This was the first time any of them had initiated the throat grabbing, and he felt himself almost explode too soon. He pulled his hands away and backed off.

"Not yet," he said. He wasn't ready yet.

Amanda smiled and said, "It's okay, I climaxed twice already."

She took his hands, again placing them at her throat, and moaned as she moved her hips underneath him. He moaned in so much pleasure. He hadn't felt this sexually pleased in a long time. He would be sad to see her go. ***Do it you, fucking pussy. Go ahead and just do it. She wants you to do it. She's practically begging you to do it. Kill the whore. She is a whore, nothing more and nothing less***. The evil seized him then, taking over his thoughts, taking over his body. His hands grew tighter around her neck, and she winced at the pressure. He pushed himself deeper and harder into her. She cried out again, but this time there was no pleasure in her cry.

"Ouch," she managed to get out before his hands were completely around her neck, full strength, full pressure, crushing her windpipe.

She whimpered beneath him, writhing under him, kicking and digging her fingernails into his back. *Kill the bitch, kill the whore, kill the bitch, kill the whore.* The evil taunted him, chanting to him, cheering him on. He came just then and, just like the others, as he came he squeezed the last bit of breath from her. Her eyes popped open so wide, so empty. He cried out as she went limp, a mixture of surprise and pleasure. *Noooo*, he thought. *I really didn't want to kill her. Maybe she would have wanted to be with me*, he thought. He looked at her. The eyes were always the same...so empty, so shallow, no feelings there once they were dead. A tear ran down his cheek. *I didn't mean to kill her really*, he thought. He had really liked her. *She was nothing but a whore. Whores don't deserve to live. You got what you wanted from her. You got her soul. She has nothing to live for anyways. She wouldn't have been for you. She would have cheated on you, left you standing all alone. I am here for you, you fucking idiot. Not her. Not anyone but me*. He shook all over. He looked at her again, her empty eyes and her breathless body. He sat as the evil screamed in his head, the sweat pouring off his skin. He didn't stop the evil this time, he didn't bother to try to make it go away. He let the evil take him. He was too weak to fight. He was spent. He didn't have the energy to fight back. *The knife Bobby, take the knife. Remember how good it felt in your hands. Take it. Do it. Show the whore who you are really after. She meant nothing to you. NOTHING! TAKE THE KNIFE AND DO IT NOW!* Bobby grabbed the knife and straddled Amanda, listening to the evil, his eyes blank. He did what the evil told him to do. He was no longer in control. He was just the body that carried the evil demon, doing its will. As he began to cut he thought to himself, *I am ready for her*.

CHAPTER THIRTY-ONE

ALEX WALKED INTO THE CAFE, READY FOR HER MORNING fix. It was over a week since her last visit to the cate, and she couldn't wait for Amanda to hook her up with her delicious morning cup of hot caffeine. She looked around and saw all the regular people sitting around, some laughing and talking over coffee, some on their laptops or reading papers. She walked over to the counter and looked around for Amanda. A young kid with messy brown hair, wire rimmed glasses, and a face full of red, cystic acne looked back at her, unsmiling.

"Can I help you?" he asked in a tone that told Alex that he didn't really want to be here, and he didn't really want to help her.

"Um, hi, where is Amanda?" Alex asked, trying to sound as nice as possible, even though she felt like telling the kid that if he didn't like his job he should just quit.

"She didn't show up this morning. The boss called her, and she didn't answer her phone. So, here I am. I hate mornings," he grumbled, as if Alex hadn't already figured that out.

"I can tell," Alex replied stiffly. She wondered if Amanda was okay. She remembered the scars on her wrists.

"Does she not show up a lot?" Alex asked, knowing she was way overstepping and going from just a concerned customer to a nosy pain in the rear.

"No, actually, she is always here. At least, she has been since I have known her. But, I am not sure I am supposed to be telling you that," he said, almost indignantly. He seemed a little uneasy after he answered, as if he had thought about it while he was talking and decided not to say anymore. His eyes shifted around to see if anyone had been listening. When he was satisfied that no one had heard them, he turned back to her, looking a little impatient now.

"What can I get you?" he asked.

"I'll just have a medium hot coffee with some milk and two sugars," she answered.

She watched as the kid worked slowly behind the corner and longed for Amanda to hurry back from whatever journey she was on. The kid finally came to the register and started to punch in the numbers.

"Two dollars and fifty cents," he said.

She noticed he hadn't said "please," and wondered how long he had been working here. She figured it hadn't been too long and, if it had, she hoped it wouldn't be much longer.

"Here," she said curtly.

She handed him the money and realized how silly she was being by thinking like that about the kid. He was probably nice in the afternoons. Maybe he just wasn't a morning person. She would be mad if she had gotten a phone call at three in the morning to come in to work for a double because someone else hadn't shown up. She snorted a little. The kid looked up at her questioningly, and she realized she had actually snorted out loud.

"Sorry," she blurted out.

Alex flashed him one of her beautiful smiles. He still stared at her, a little incredulously, and didn't offer to return her smile. She grabbed her coffee and turned to leave. *Wow, kids these days*, she thought. She giggled again, thinking she sounded like Abuela.

She walked out of the cafe and headed towards home. It was still dark, no sign of the sun peaking out anywhere. *It's pretty early still,* she thought. She had started her run an hour earlier than she normally did. She walked slowly, enjoying the heat from her coffee cup as it warmed her hands. She hummed a little tune to herself as she walked, thinking that she might get dressed and go into work early today. She had started seeing patients again, and her appointments had been filling up. If she went in early, she could take the extra time to do some paperwork before her first appointment came in.

As she turned the corner, she noticed the dark shadow of a car parked on the side of the road near one of the abandoned parking lots she usually walked by. No lights were on in the car, and it didn't seem to be running, as far as she could tell. She could just make out that the hood of the car was propped up. *Ah, man*, she thought, *not a good time or great weather to have car problems*. As she got closer she wondered if she should cross the street to the other side before she got too close. Just then, she saw a man coming out from underneath the hood. He was dressed all in black, and one of his arms appeared to be shorter than the other. She walked a few more feet before realizing his left arm was in a sling. *Crap*, she thought, *bad weather, bad arm, bad timing*. She walked up to the man.

"Hey, sir, do you need....?" she started to say. She trailed off as she realized that she knew the guy.

"Hey," she exclaimed.

It was the guy from the cafe. But something lurched in her stomach, and she thought for a second she might lose the coffee she had just consumed. A sick feeling came over her, and she froze only a foot from the man. It was the guy from the cafe, but it was also………

"Well, hello there, Alex. I have been waiting to meet you up close for a very long time." He smiled at her warmly, but nothing about him felt warm to her. She was frozen in fear. Her feet felt glued to the ground as if two cinder blocks were glued to the bottoms of her shoes. Her mind raced, thinking of all the things she should be doing: running, screaming, flailing. But she couldn't do anything except stand there staring at him in disbelief. Then he moved, just slightly, and she realized why he had his arm in a sling. The moonlight glinted off the metal, something black and shiny inside his sling. She could just make out the tip of the barrel of a hand gun.

"Did you like the flowers I sent you?" he asked, speaking as if he were holding a regular conversation with a friend or a lover. She stood there, breathless, not moving. He appeared to become agitated.

"I *said*, did you like the flowers I sent you?" This time a little louder.

"I, um, I…" she stumbled. He smiled again, seemingly tickled by her inability to speak.

"I know. You must be a little confused. But don't worry, I am going to clarify everything for you in a little while. First we have to take a little ride." He pointed towards the black car.

Alex still didn't move. She *couldn't* move. She couldn't speak. She couldn't run or scream. She could barely breathe. Suddenly, before she knew what was happening, he grabbed her by the arm making her drop her coffee on the ground. She winced in pain. He was extremely strong. His hands seemed as if they could encircle her arm twice over. He shoved her over towards the car, pushing the butt of the gun into her rib cage. All of a sudden, the trunk of the car popped open on its own. He must have the keys in his hand, she thought.

"Inside," he ordered.

Oh god, not inside the trunk, she shuddered. Her eyes grew big, and she looked frantically between him and the trunk of the car.

"Inside," he said again patiently, almost as if he were speaking to a child who wasn't hearing him correctly. He motioned to the trunk while at the same time nudging her in the ribs with the gun again.

She felt as if she were going to vomit. She looked at him once more, waiting for him to say or do something, but he just pointed to the trunk again. Reluctantly, she climbed into the trunk and curled her body up, trying to somehow protect herself. She wondered if anyone could see them or hear them. At five in the morning not many people were up roaming around. Not many people other than the two of them. He looked at her for a moment to make sure she was comfortable and shut the trunk door with a thud. Alex lay in the dark for a few minutes in near silence. The only sound in the dark tomb of the trunk was her quick, shallow breathing. She had a split second where she imagined herself suffocating in there. *Stop it! You have to stay calm. If not, you will hyperventilate and pass out. Then what good will you be?* She willed herself to take a few deep breaths and tried to allow her eyes to adjust to the dark. She heard some noises outside the trunk, a slamming noise and a slight shake of the car. He must have closed the hood of the car, she thought. Then, a few seconds later, there was the creak of the car door. The car slumped and sagged a little under his weight, and she heard the door slam. She lay there, breathing. *At least I am breathing*, she thought. The sound of the ignition made her jump. The trunk was cold, but she had already started to sweat. A bead fell into her eye and stung her.

She tried to blink it away. It was so cramped in here. *This is what it must be like to get buried alive*, she thought. Again, she had to will herself away from thinking those kinds of things. She had to think of other things, like how to get the hell away from this guy. Just then she felt the car lurch forward, and they were moving... to where, she did not know.

CHAPTER THIRTY-TWO

"911... THIS CALL IS BEING RECORDED. PLEASE STATE YOUR emergency?" the dispatcher answered.

"I live at 443 Lake Street, and I just found a…. the body of my neighbor. I think her name is Amanda. I was walking down the hall-way leaving for work, and I….you know, the door was wide open. So I looked in to make sure she was okay, like to tell her, "Hey, your door is open," and there she was…. Oh, my god…." The caller blubbered into the phone trying to catch her breath between sobs.

"Okay, try to calm down, ma'am. Is your neighbor moving, speaking, conscious?" the dispatcher asked efficiently.

"Nooo..!!" the woman whined into the phone.

"Okay, calm down and try to tell me, is your neighbor still alive? Is she still breathing?" the dispatcher asked.

"I… I don't think so, she has blood on her and…. Oh, god, please just send someone now… please." The woman on the phone sobbed again.

The dispatcher could tell she was trying to hold it together but wasn't sure how much longer she was going to be able to keep her on the phone.

"Okay, we are going to send over a car. Please stay on the phone with me until officers arrive, okay?" the dispatcher asked.

"Um, okay, but I, oh, okay." The voice trailed off a bit.

The dispatcher picked up the radio and called for the closest unit in the area.

"I need a squad car and ambo over to 443 Lake Street, for an 'unattended'," she called over the radio.

A voice crackled over the intercom calling back affirmation, and she replaced the radio into its cradle. She returned to the phone where the caller waited.

"Ma'am, are you still there?" the dispatcher asked.

"Y-yes, I'm still here," sniffled the witness.

"Okay, just stay on the line with me. I have a car and an ambulance in route. They should be there in a few minutes. Just hang on the line with me until they get there. Okay?" the dispatcher tried to sound as nice as she could, using her most soothing voice. She had never seen anyone hurt before and couldn't imagine what it did to your mind.

"Okay, I'm here. I will stay on until the cops come," the caller answered back, starting to sound a bit calmer.

The dispatcher smiled to herself. *Thank God I was able to calm her down a little,* she thought. There were many days that calls didn't always end so well. It made it hard to do her job sometimes. These were the calls that made it worthwhile. The dispatcher sat back in her chair and relaxed a bit as she heard the faint sound of sirens on the other line.

"Okay, ma'am, I hear the sirens. Do you see the police?" the dispatcher asked sweetly.

"Yeah," the woman sighed.

"Alright. They can take it from here. Thank you for your help. Good luck." And with that, the dispatcher ended the call.

The woman on the other end stood looking at her cell phone for a moment, listening to the faint sound of the dial tone. After a moment, the dead man's busy signal began to beep. *How ironic,* thought the woman, before killing the sound with the snapping shut of her phone. She turned and walked toward the sound of the sirens.

CHAPTER THIRTY-THREE

ALEX WAS STARTING TO FEEL LIKE SHE COULDN'T breathe again. Her head was pounding, and her stomach was as queasy as if she had just ridden the worst roller coaster in history a million times. She had to keep swallowing hard to keep down the coffee and bile that was trying to force its way out of her esophagus. Her eyes had gotten used to the dark in the trunk, so she was able to see some of her surroundings thanks to a small hole in the metal of the car.

It must be getting light out, she thought. She wasn't sure how much time had passed, but it already seemed like an eternity. She swallowed again. She tried to turn over to a different position, but she was so cramped in there, it was difficult to move. She could feel the car turning what must have been left, then turning what could have been right, and then stopping for what had to have been a red light. She tried kicking the truck lid and screaming, but to no avail. All she managed to do was make her feet sore and her head hurt, because her screams went nowhere but into her own ears.

Suddenly, she felt the car stop again. She waited, wondering if they were at another light. She soon realized they must be wherever they were going because the car's engine was no longer running. She stayed very still for a few moments, waiting, trying to listen. She could hear some movements. She felt the car spring upwards a little, and she thought he must have gotten out. Then the car door slammed shut. She waited, her body coiled tight as a spring rod. She could hear her breath coming in short, shallow huffs, as if she were listening to someone else, breathing. She thought she might try to swing her leg out and kick him in the face when he opened the trunk, catching him by surprise.

Alex waited, poised, ready to flail at him. But he didn't come. She wondered what he was doing. She couldn't hear anything outside the car. She finally gave up the idea of kicking him and tried to relax her body. Her muscles ached, and her head felt as if someone had stepped on it repeatedly. She laid her head down on the floor of the trunk and closed her eyes. Suddenly she was so tired...exhausted, actually...more tired than she had ever felt in her life. *The adrenaline must be wearing off,* she thought. She was starting to shiver a little, thinking how cold it had gotten in the last few weeks. She wrapped her arms around herself and curled back up into the fetal position.

Just as she was about to doze off, a rumbling sound startled her eyes open. It was as if a fleet of jet fighter planes were just overhead, the sound so loud it almost deafened her. The car shook like a small earthquake was rocking it. Then she realized what it was...a train. She must be close to some kind of train tracks, she thought. She pulled her hands up over her ears, pushing her fingertips into each ear hole to muffle the roaring sound until it passed. When it finally diminished, she pulled her arms back around herself and tried to warm herself. She laid her head back down and closed her eyes.

CHAPTER THIRTY-FOUR

MANNY AND DESHAWN ARRIVED AT THE APARTMENT AN hour after the call came in. There were already a few uniformed police officers there, as well as the CSI unit. Lights flashed all around them as they came in the doorway, as if they had just made their grand entrance onto the red carpet. CSI agents were taking pictures of everything in sight and dusting for fingerprints while uniformed officers stood guard at the front door. Manny looked over and saw a white sheet pulled over a body, a few spots of blood already seeping through the thick white sheet creating a bloody misshapen ghost face. He walked over to the body and was just about to pull the sheet down when Dickerson, the head CSI guy, stopped him.

"Hey, Manny, wait a minute. I have to talk to you first," he said.

Manny looked at him, puzzled. He figured Dickerson just wanted to go over some of the details of the crime with him. Manny pulled his hand back and stood up, waiting for Dickerson to say something. He seemed to be stalling a little, trying to find the words, and Manny wondered what the hell was going on.

"The victim's name is Amanda, a Caucasian female, aged twenty-three. The neighbor found her. The front door had been left wide open." He paused for a minute looking at Manny.

Manny didn't know what his problem was, but he had better just spit it out. He was getting irritated.

"Okay, so we know some of that already. What is the real issue, Dickerson?" he asked curtly.

Dickerson looked at him again, something in his eyes. Manny wasn't sure he liked what he saw... hesitation, maybe.

"Well, Manny, I just wanted you to be prepared before you took a look at her. It seems whoever killed her knows Alex," he said, studying Manny's face.

Manny stood there for a moment, then abruptly ripped the sheet off the body. He looked at the victim's chest with wide eyes. A slight moan escaped his lips.

The victim was lying on her back, her eyes wide open. Her chest and stomach were exposed. Whatever clothes she had been wearing had been either ripped or cut open and had fallen down to her sides. But none of these things were what caught Manny's attention. His eyes were transfixed on her bare breasts and stomach where something had been carved into her skin. The letters were mismatched in size, but they were still legible, caked with scabbing blood. They read "Alex Aguilar"...two words engraved into the delicate, pale flesh of this young girl who lay before them. Manny swallowed hard. He could feel a bead of sweat run down his spine. His heart began to pound, and he fumbled in his pocket for his cell phone.

He dialed Alex's cell phone number and let it ring seven times, not waiting for the voicemail to pick up. He tried her home number, letting it ring ten times before he hung up. He tried her cell again, and then her home number again. He looked at his watch. Ten a.m. He called the office. It rang three times before Lola picked up.

"Thank you for calling….." she began.

Manny cut her off before she could finish.

"Lola, it's Manny. Is Alex there?" he asked, trying not to sound desperate.

"No, Mr. Manny. I was actually just about to call her. Her ten thirty appointment is already here, and I just wanted to make sure she was on her way. Mr. Manny, is everything okay? You sound funny," she asked, sounding a little worried at his abrupt tone.

"I don't know, Lola. It's probably nothing, but have Alex call me as soon as she gets in or when you get a hold of her on the phone. Tell her it's important, okay?" he said.

"Sure, Mr. Manny, I will do that," she said.

Manny hung up the phone before she got a chance to say goodbye.

"Manny?" Deshawn looked at him concerned. "Are you okay?" he asked.

Manny looked at him, his brow furrowed.

"She's not answering, and Lola says she isn't at work," he told him.

Deshawn looked at Manny, watching his eyes for a moment. He saw the flashes of anger and worry blaze there.

"Well, let's go over to her house," Deshawn said.

"I was just thinking that," Manny responded.

He put his cell phone back into his pocket and looked at Dickerson.

"I will call Lopez and Jackson and have them come take over here. We have to get out of here and go check on Alex."

Dickerson looked at Manny and nodded, his face showing concern. They all knew Alex, and it was hard when one of their own was being targeted. They also knew how much Alex meant to Manny, although no one dared speak the words.

"I will help them take care of the situation over here, Manny. Just go and find Alex, and keep her safe," Dickerson answered.

He patted Manny on the shoulder before turning away to hand out instructions to his team.

"Okay, Deshawn, let's go." Manny turned quickly, already heading toward the door.

Deshawn followed behind him, feeling the tension emanating from Manny's body. Deshawn felt a sickening feeling as the image of the girl's body leaped into his mind again. He brushed it away and focused on Manny's back. He didn't say anything on the way out of the apartment. He knew, right now, less was better.

CHAPTER THIRTY-FIVE

ALEX'S CHEST FELT HEAVY, AS IF SOMEONE WAS SITTING on it. She wasn't sure how long she had been locked in the dark trunk, but she had counted the train going by thirteen times. She didn't know if it ran every hour or every half hour, but she figured that she had been in there for at least ten hours. She couldn't hear much of anything besides the rumbling of the train when it passed. The trunk seemed to be well insulated. She wondered if he had made it that way on purpose. One thing she was sure of, he had been planning this for a long time. Her eyes hurt from trying to adjust to the darkness, and her lips were chapped. Thirst nagged her dry mouth and throat, and her frozen skin begged to be heated. She found a small blanket that had been pushed into a corner of the trunk and covered up with it. It did little to warm her from the cold air that seeped through the steel of the car. She thought she might freeze to death if she stayed here too long. She shuddered at the thought. So many ruminations had already gone through her mind. Why had she told Manny to go home? Why hadn't the cops been able to stay just a few days longer? Why did this madman decide to pick on her? The cold and frustration shook her body intensely.

She was deep in thought, her eyes closed and arms wrapped around her, when the trunk popped open. Before she knew what was happening, a large hand reached in and covered her mouth with a wet cloth. Her eyes popped open, but they were unable to focus. A sweet smell filled her nostrils and, before she could stop herself, she was trying to gasp for air and sucking in whatever was soaked into the cloth. It burned her nostrils and throat, but as soon as she felt the burning, she felt nothing else.

Darkness took over, and her eyes closed. Her breathing stabilized, and Bobby watched as her body fell limp. He smiled. He took a moment to look from her to the surrounding area and, once he was satisfied that no one was around, reached into the trunk to pick her up. Her body was dead weight, but he still lifted her easily.

Bobby closed the trunk a little clumsily and walked towards the abandoned warehouse. He walked through a doorway that was missing its door, and continued walking down the dark hallway. He could hear the wind whistling through the broken windows, and papers rustled on the dirty floor. Occasionally, he stepped on something and heard the crunching sounds it made under the weight of his boots echo through the empty hallways. He continued deep into the heart of the building, abandoned for many years, and brought her into the area that he had readied for her. He was sure that the small room had served as the foreman's office at one point. It was the only room that had all the plexiglass left in its window panes...the thick kind that was probably shatter and sound proof. He imagined that many people had been hired and fired in this room. He carried her over to the twin mattress he had bought from the Salvation Army store a few weeks ago. It had a few stains of it, their origins he had not wanted to imagine. He had purchased some sheets and a blanket to make it somewhat new for her. He placed her on the mattress, almost dropping her, huffing from the work. Dust billowed up around them from the movement, and he sneezed violently. He cursed out loud, and it echoed in the small room . Alex moaned a little and rolled over on the bed. He looked at her for a moment, making sure she was still out, before he turned to survey the room.

He had also purchased a battery operated camping lantern from the camping section of the local K-Mart. A low hum emanated from its glow as it sat, stoic in the corner on a dilapidated desk that had been left behind. Bobby covered her with the K-Mart blue light special twin sized comforter. It was covered in Power Puff Girls displayed in various fighting positions, exchanging blows with evildoers who were trying to take over Townsville. Bobby went over and sat in the chair that stood next to the broken desk. It squeaked as he sat, rolling slightly to the left when he plunked himself down. He figured it wasn't designed to hold someone of his size, but it held steady. The arms of the chair were wobbly, and they gave way a bit to accommodate his size. The room was cold, and he watched his breath, little white clouds, emerging from his lips. He had brought some extra clothes and blankets for her, also. He didn't want her freezing to death before he could have his time with her. He knew the clothes would be too big, but they would do the trick.

He watched her again, feeling warm and tingly inside. *I have finally gotten her. I have finally gotten the prize.* He knew once she woke she would be fighting mad, but he was hoping over time she would grow to like him. He would just have to use his charm on her, that's all. He wasn't sure how long the chloroform would work, but he decided he could leave for now. He left the lamp on. He had made sure to put brand new batteries in so that she would have light for the next twenty four hours or so. He had also brought a few bottles of water, some granola bars, a large paint bucket she could use as a toilet, and some books for her to read. He thought she was going to be quite comfortable here. He smiled again. He hadn't felt this elated in a very long time. He made sure the extra blankets were near her for when she woke so that she didn't get too cold. He blew her sleeping body a kiss and closed the heavy metal door behind him. He had replaced the old, wooden door with the fire-proof metal one a few weeks ago. He took out his keys and locked the door. He took one last glance at her through the blurry window, then turned to head out.

CHAPTER THIRTY-SIX

MANNY AND DESHAWN WERE IN THE CAR DRIVING BACK to the station. It was getting dark, and the thermometer in the car read twenty-seven degrees. Manny drove in silence, his eyes fixed on the road ahead. The lights flew by them, and Deshawn watched as they reflected off the windshield, making a strange yellow strobe light in the car. Deshawn yawned deeply. He watched Manny for a few minutes before he spoke.

"I think we should go ahead and release the information to the press," Deshawn said, shrinking into his seat a little.

He waited for the explosion from Manny, who had been on edge since they had been at Alex's house and hadn't found her there. They had called Lola every hour or so since, with no luck. Lola stayed at the office until five p.m., waiting to see if Alex would show up. But they all knew something was not right when she didn't show up that morning. The last time Manny spoke to Lola, he had to console her and send her home. She had been crying all afternoon, and Manny had to coerce her into leaving. He finally managed to get her to leave the office on the promise that he would call her as soon as he knew anything.

Manny took a deep breath in and seemed to think for a minute before answering Deshawn.

"I think you're probably right. I am also going to call in the Deployment Team and have them start a search and rescue." Manny's voice trembled a little with his last few words.

Deshawn knew Manny was burning up inside. Deshawn also felt as if something was eating away at him. They had to find Alex. They just had to.

"When we get back, I will make a call to Grace Dipilato and fill her in on what we have so far. They should be able to run it on the eleven o'clock news if I get to her soon," Deshawn said.

"I am going to have the Deployment Team revisit all the addresses we have on this Bobby Benson, Jr., and see if they can't come up with something. I wish we had a little more on this guy," Manny said.

He looked older to Deshawn under the alternating flashing yellow lights and the darkness of the car. He was sunken down into the driver's seat, his shoulders slumped, and Deshawn thought that he must feel like he had been run over by a truck.

They sat in silence for the next fifteen minutes until they pulled into the station. Manny slammed on the brakes when he arrived at his parking spot, and Deshawn had to put his hand out onto the dashboard to keep from flying into the windshield.

"Shit, Manny!" he yelped.

Under different circumstances, this would have elicited a booming laugh from Manny. He was forever telling Deshawn to put his seat belt on, to no avail. The large, former linebacker seemed to have "invincibilitis." Instead, it earned him a quick sideways glance and a somewhat sincere apology.

"Sorry, man. I just need to get this going, ya know?" Manny said, already out of the car. Deshawn had to hurry to catch up with him.

"Look, Manny, I know how you are feeling, but wait up. Don't leave me behind here, buddy. We are going to find her together."

Deshawn had to jog to catch up with Manny. Manny didn't turn around to wait for him, and he didn't respond. He just kept walking as fast as he could towards the parking garage's elevator. Deshawn sighed, undeterred, and stayed right on Manny's heels. He knew Manny was a stubborn man, but this was going to be the hardest case they had ever worked together.

The elevator wasn't moving fast enough for him. Manny pushed the number three button several times, growing more and more impatient as the seconds ticked by. Deshawn stood behind him in silence. Manny felt a little guilty for ignoring him in the parking garage, but he had to focus right now. He had to put all his thoughts into where Alex could be. He already knew who had her, and he had to find him in order to find her. *I am coming, Alex*, he thought. *I am coming to get you.*

CHAPTER THIRTY-SEVEN

ALEX WOKE UP COUGHING, COLD, AND EXTREMELY confused. The room was unfamiliar to her, and she had to force herself to focus. She sat up and looked around her. It was a small room that appeared to be an old office of some sort. She was sitting on a twin mattress that had what appeared to be a young girl's comforter on it. There was an old broken down desk in the corner of the room with a tattered old chair on wheels. The only light came from a battery powered lamp that sat on top of the broken desk. It buzzed a hello to her when she looked at it. She saw a box in the corner with some material that looked like clothing in it. A small cooler sat next to it. She looked around again, making sure there was no one here with her, before she stood to walk over to the box. Her body ached all over, and the muscles in her legs shook under her weight. She felt like she had run a marathon.

Alex shuffled over to the box and bent over, pulling out what looked like a pair of sweatpants. They were definitely too big for her, but she didn't care. She slowly put her sneakers through the holes of the pants and pulled them up over the other pair of thin running pants that she had worn out that morning. She grabbed a sweatshirt from the same box, also too big, and pulled it over her head. The clothes smelled musty, but she didn't care. They would help keep her warm.

She leaned over and pushed the top of the cooler off to reveal some bottled waters and granola bars. She quickly grabbed a bottle of water and ripped off the cap as fast as she could, gulping down the cold liquid, thinking that she never loved the taste of water so much. She grabbed a granola bar, not even bothering to see what kind it was, and sat back down on the tattered mattress to eat.

Alex looked around again, this time more slowly and focused. She noticed that the glass that filled the panes on the window of the door looked thick, and she could imagine that she wasn't going to be able to break it. But as soon as she had a little more energy, she sure as hell was going to try. The door looked like it was made of metal. *Probably fire proof or something*, she thought. *Well, this guy had really planned and thought this all out,* she sighed. A new wave of dread crashed through her, threatening to knock her down. The tears began to fall again as she forced herself to continue eating the granola bar, even though she couldn't taste it anymore. The only things she could taste were fear and terror as they engulfed her. *At least*, she thought, *I am still alive and, if he had planned on killing me, he certainly isn't going to do it yet. Otherwise, he wouldn't have left me food, water, and things to keep warm.* But what did that mean was in store for her in the next few hours, next few days, or even weeks. *Oh, god*, she shuddered, thinking of the trail of victims he had already left for them. Unable to continue to imagine any of the things he could do to her, Alex laid back onto the mattress, covered herself with all of the blankets, and tried to think of a way out of the nightmare she was in.

CHAPTER THIRTY-EIGHT

BOBBY LAY IN HIS BED WATCHING THE ELEVEN O'CLOCK news. He was eager to see if they had put out any information on the now missing Dr. Alex Aguilar. It was getting late, and he was tired, his eyes growing heavy from lack of sleep. He had worked very hard making sure everything was just right. His eyes were nearly shut when he sat up suddenly, shocked that he saw a much younger picture of himself splashed on the screen. It was the picture of him when he was locked up in the juvenile detention center. Then another picture of him flashed on the screen, this one was from the driver's license that he had given to Stella when he applied at the cable company. *What the fuck?* The anchor woman, Grace Dipilato, was saying something about him. He had to focus to make out what she was saying, his mind muddled with fear and shock. *Shit, did she just use my real name*?? His heart jumped into his throat as he listened….

"Police detectives are asking for your help tonight in the disappearance of Dr. Alexandra Aguilar. They have identified this man, Robert Benson, Jr. as a person of interest in the disappearance. It is believed that this man goes by many different names and could be

anywhere right now. It is also believed that this man may be armed and dangerous. Police also informed us that Mr. Benson is wanted for information in connection with four other murders that have occurred in the last five months, including the murder of Ms. Bowen, ex-wife of prominent lawyer Mr. John Bowen. This also includes the latest murder of a young woman found early this morning. The police have issued a reward for any information leading to the arrest of the man they are now calling 'The Grafton Hill Strangler'.....''

The woman continued talking, but Bobby couldn't listen any longer. *They have my real name and my real face on television.* He had thought it would take longer for them to find out about him, that he would have a lot more time with her before they actually knew who he was. ***You fucking idiot. Of course, they know who you are, you dumb bastard. You left too many clues. You were too careless, you dumb fuck. You were clumsy like you always have been. I warned you to be more careful, but you let your excitement get the better of you,*** the evil screamed at him.

He wasn't surprised when the evil came anymore. He expected it to come when it did. He almost welcomed it. He had been allowing it to take control more often now. It kept him from dealing with every-thing. *The evil is saving me,* he thought. It didn't matter that it screamed at him and said bad things to him. He deserved it; he always had. ***You need to get rid of the bitch. She is going to make it so that you will never see the sun again. She will get you in a lot of trouble. Hell, you are already in a lot of trouble. You need to get rid of her, and then you need to disappear. You really fucked things up this time, asshole.*** The evil was right. He had really gotten himself into trouble this time. He was going to have to run again, just like he always did. He had left too many prints of himself here, too many victims, too many clues. He was going to have to take care of Alex soon, but not before he could spend a little one on one time with her. He smiled as he thought of it. He felt himself growing hard in excitement, but he tried to push it away. He wanted to save himself for her. He didn't want to waste it on fantasy. He wanted to save it for the real thing...her. He turned off the television and laid down on the bed. He knew he had to get some sleep and build up his energy for the next few days that he would be spending with her. He knew they might be his last few days, but they were definitely going to be her last.

CHAPTER THIRTY-NINE

ALEX SHIVERED UNDER THE BLANKETS, A COMBINATION of cold and fear. The tears had dried up a few hours ago, and now she lay limp and tired but could not sleep. She had no idea what time it was, if it was day or night. *At least I still have the lamp.* She had gotten up a while ago needing to pee, but wasn't sure what to do until she found the bucket in the corner with crude black letters painted on its side..."toilet." She shuddered in disgust, but decided that it was either use the bucket or use her pants. Dignity was not something she could afford in a place like this, so she settled for the bucket. The cold air smacked her skin when she pulled her pants down to hover over the bucket. She felt violated and ashamed. She figured that was how a caged animal must feel.

Alex returned to the mattress and lay looking at the decaying ceiling. She could see that it used to be white, but over the years it had yellowed and was stained with water spots that formed menacing, disfigured faces staring down at her. She had figured out she was in some kind of office, but where it was located, she did not know. Her head still pounded, and her body still ached. She had already tried some of her own psychological training on herself, trying to talk to herself, to calm and soothe herself, but nothing worked. She was still here in this freezing room, being held captive by a man she knew hardly anything about, except that he was capable of horrific things. No amount of coping mechanisms was going to help her feel safe or warm.

Okay, girl, get it together. She rubbed her eyes with the backs of her cold hands and sat up. Alex took a deep breath in and began to look around. She wondered when Bobby would return and grew determined at the thought. She focused on looking around, taking inventory of every little thing in the room, and hunting for anything that she might be able to use against her kidnapper as a weapon. There was nothing in the room that looked sharp to stab him with. There was the old, rusty chair. Maybe she could try to slam the chair against the glass and break it. She wasn't sure if she had enough energy to even pick up the chair in that moment. But she realized that if she didn't do something, she would not make it out alive. She got up and walked over to the chair, but when she lifted it above her head, her arms shook from its weight. She quickly put it back down, realizing she would probably not have the strength to throw it at the windows. She went to the windows, trying to decide which one she should aim for. She didn't care, any one of them. She had to try again. So she went back to the chair, mustered up all the energy she could, and heaved it as hard as she could towards the glass. The chair hit the window with a thud and actually bounced back towards her. Alex had to move quickly to get out of its way. *It must be reinforced glass, like plexiglass,* she thought. Not even a small crack was visible where the chair had struck. Just a few nicks in the glass told the story of the chair. Alex sighed and felt a surge of anger welling up inside of her. Her face felt hot, and her breath came quick. She looked around the room more frantically. She had to find something before he came back.

Alex looked up at the ceiling again, more closely this time, for an air duct. She spotted one in the corner, and her heart skipped a beat. *Okay, now how do I get there?* She looked around for the abused chair. She grabbed it, placed it directly under the air duct, and climbed on gingerly. She wobbled on the wheeled chair, arms out to keep her balance like a tightrope walker, all while trying to gauge the distance to the air duct. Alex carefully reached her hand up towards the edge of the air duct, but her fingertips just barely grazed it.

"Damn it!" she yelled.

She tried again, reaching, stretching her body as far as she could, the chair rolling slightly beneath her. Alex could feel herself losing balance, but she had to try and reach the duct. It could be her only way out. She stretched just a little further and, when she did, the chair rolled out from beneath her, and she fell. She landed on the cold concrete on her side, banging her hip and scraping her elbow. Alex called out as a flash of pain flew through her. She lay there a moment on the cold dusty floor, the pain radiating down her side. Her mind tried hard to focus and work, but suddenly she felt so cloudy and muddled. She finally gave up and slowly dragged herself back to the mattress. She lay there, resigned for now. Alex laid her head back and waited.

CHAPTER FORTY

MANNY SAT AT HIS DESK STARING AT THE PICTURE OF Bobby Benson, Jr., on the computer screen. He absentmindedly squeezed his hand into a fist and then let it go, over and over again, his knuckles shining white at the pressure with which he made his fist. He had been there all night making phone calls and intercepting radio transmissions from the Deployment Team. They hadn't found much of anything since he sent them out. They had gone over the streets that were Alex's running roads and had found a half empty coffee cup, from the same cafe Alex always went to, discarded in the road. When he had gotten the news, Manny's heart had sunk into his stomach. He just knew that the cup was from Alex. That was her routine. They sent the cup over to the lab to see if they could pull fingerprints off of it. Manny was waiting on the results, even though he knew that Alex's fingerprints were going to be there. He was glad now that a few years ago the department had made anyone assisting Homicide be fingerprinted and give sample DNA after one of their snitches had been found murdered and nearly unidentifiable.

Manny continued to stare blankly at the picture of the man on his computer screen, ignoring the ringing phones in the cubicles around him and the rising noise of people chattering as other detectives started to shuffle in for the first shift of the day. He looked out of his window and watched as the sun began to peak over the horizon to say good morning. The sun was trying hard to poke through the billowy clouds that swam in the sky, and it cast a purple color upon them, making for a brilliant sunrise. Normally, he loved it when he had late nights and could sit there to enjoy the sunrise with a nice hot cup of coffee. This morning, though, the break of day only reminded him that the hands on the clock were still ticking and, the more they ticked, the less time he had to find Alex. He sighed and inhaled deeply. His eyes were damp, and he jabbed at them, hastily wiping away the tears so that no one would notice he had been crying. He had sent Deshawn home to his family at two a.m. He had argued with Manny for a little while, but had finally given in when he realized that Manny wasn't going to change his mind. Deshawn left with the promise that he would return first thing in the morning.

Manny turned around in his chair as the fax machine announced incoming information. He hoped it was going to be the information he wanted from the Texas prison system. He had called late last night and requested the records of any and all visitors to one Robert Benson, Sr., in the last fifteen years. The warden told Manny he would have his people hop right on it, but Manny wasn't sure how sincere he had been, seeing as how he had insisted the warden be awakened in the middle of the night. Manny had apologized profusely, using the lame excuse that he had forgotten about the time difference between them.

Manny pulled the sheet of paper out of the fax and swept his eyes over the information. There were very few names on the list, and the last visitor had come over nine years ago. The names there were that of the prisoner's mother, sister, and a cousin that visited only once. Bobby, Jr.'s, name was nowhere to be found. Manny didn't feel disappointed. He felt it wasn't going to lead anywhere anyway. He had figured the kid wasn't going to visit his murdering father, except maybe in an attempt to kill him. That wasn't going to happen in a maximum security prison. Bobby, Sr., had been moved to minimum security five years ago, but no one had been to see him there.

Manny threw the paper onto his desk and took a sip of his cold black coffee. He winced a little, not realizing how long he had let it sit there to get cold, and resisted the temptation to spit it back out into the cup. He swallowed hard and decided to get a warm cup. As he stood, Deshawn came into the office and spotted him, shaking his head.

"I know, I know," Manny said. He knew what Deshawn was thinking before he even said anything.

"I haven't been home yet, and I'm not planning on going home until I find something out about Alex." He turned and walked away from Deshawn.

Deshawn followed him to the coffee pot. Manny's clothes were wrinkled, and his hair was slightly disheveled. What Deshawn noticed most, however, were the dark circles that were set deep into the skin beneath Manny's eyes.

"I'm not gonna say anything except that maybe you could use a few hours of sleep, that's all," Deshawn retorted.

Normally, he would feel a little hurt by Manny's curtness, but he had already prepared himself. He knew Manny was not going to be himself until Alex was home safe.

"Yeah, well, I am going to take a hit of this motor oil here and get back to work," Manny said, as he poured himself another cup of coffee. Deshawn smiled a little at Manny's back.

"Well, at least go brush your dirty grill," Deshawn said as Manny turned around. He held out a plastic zip lock bag containing a new toothbrush, a small tube of toothpaste, a bar of soap, and a disposable razor. Manny smiled a little.

"What's the matter? You don't like my gator breath?" Manny asked with a grunt.

"It wasn't my idea, it was Muriel's. She also sent some muffins, Italian grinders, and leftover lasagna with me. She said she knew it was going to be another late night, and she wanted to make sure we were well fueled," Deshawn said.

Good old Muriel, Manny thought. She was a great wife to his partner and a good friend to him. She took good care of them both. Manny grabbed the plastic goodie bag from Deshawn and passed off his coffee cup in trade. Deshawn nodded at Manny in quiet understanding and watched as he headed toward the locker rooms. Deshawn sighed as he watched him, noticing that his shoulders were still slumped, and he was walking a little slower than normal. Deshawn knew what Manny was thinking. They had to act quickly for Alex's sake. He took a deep breath and walked over to the phone that was ringing.

"Homicide, Detective Freeman."

CHAPTER FORTY-ONE

ALEX JUMPED WHEN SHE HEARD THE SOUND OF A KEY IN the lock, turning, clicking. The door creaked as it opened, and she shuddered, afraid to turn around. Her back was to the door, and she tried to lie as still as she could, pretending to be asleep. Heavy footsteps fell on the concrete floor, slow and methodical, growing louder. She knew he was getting close to her, and it was all she could do to stifle the scream that was building up inside her. She held her shaking hand over her mouth and willed herself to be still. She could hear him breathing. She waited, and it was quiet for a minute or two, as if he were debating what to do.

"Hello, Alex," he said.

His voice echoed slightly in the room, but it boomed in her head and crawled on her skin. She tried again with all her might not to move.

"I know you're awake. Why don't you turn over and let me have a look at you." Bobby's voice was smooth and calm, almost coaxing. If she had been in any other situation, she could imagine that she wouldn't have any trouble following his instructions. She jumped when she felt his hand on her shoulder and cried out in fear.

"No!" she screamed. She almost didn't recognize her own voice.

"Hey, hey now, I am not going to hurt you," he almost whined.

Alex whipped around to face him. She instinctively backed herself up all the way until she was touching the wall. He smiled at her, a brilliant, loving smile that made her stomach lurch in disgust.

"Oh, honey, please don't back away from me. You don't have to worry. I wouldn't hurt you. I want to enjoy you. And I want you to enjoy our time together." Again he smiled and reached out for her.

Alex couldn't go anywhere, the cold wall was holding her prisoner. She tried to shrink herself into a ball, shunning his outreached hand. He frowned at her now, and his face grew red. She could see the blood rising, like boiling water on the stove, and half expected steam to spurt from his ears. Feeling close to madness, she had to stifle the laugh that threatened to erupt from her at the image of his face on a steam pot. *This is it. I have lost it. I cannot laugh. It will only anger him more, and then who knows what he will do to me*, she thought. She wished she didn't care, she didn't want him touching her. His black eyes seared her.

"So, you want to be that way, huh? You know…" he began, then paused.

He seemed to think before he spoke, almost as if he were trying to calm himself. He sighed deeply, then continued, "I have been watching you for a while. I know that you are alone, and that you must be lonely. I only want to fill that void. I just want to be near you."

He said the last few words almost in a whisper. Alex could feel the desire emanating from him, she could smell the lust. Her mouth went dry as she watched his mouth form a smile once again, but this time the smile wasn't warm or loving. It was a twisted mess of lust, and she felt her heart sink.

"Stand up!" he demanded.

Alex lay there as still as she could, pretending that she hadn't heard anything. Her heart was pounding in her chest. She squeezed her eyes shut and tried to focus on anything but his breathing. It had gotten heavier and faster, and it sent shivers down her spine.

"I said, STAND UP!" he yelled this time, piercing her ears.

She flinched at his anger and very slowly brought herself up from the mattress. Her legs were shaking uncontrollably, and tears flowed down her face. He didn't seem to notice how frightened she was and, if he did, he didn't show it. His eyes moved up and down her body as if he were trying to see right through her clothes. Alex felt the vomit trying to work its way up into her throat. She couldn't take it anymore.

"What the hell do you want from me?" she screamed back.

Her eyes were wild with terror and fury, and just the sight of her like that drove him over the edge. He grew instantly hard and knew he was going to explode any minute now.

"Take off your clothes," he hissed.

"What?" she cried.

"I said take off your clothes." This time a little louder and with more force.

Alex couldn't believe what she was hearing. She clutched her arms around herself and stared defiantly at him. Her lips trembled. She bit her bottom lip to try to keep it from trembling any more, drawing blood. Sweat beads had started to form on his face, and she watched as his eyes again moved up and down her body. That was when she noticed his right arm behind his back. He saw her glance at his arm and smiled.

"Oh yeah, I forgot to show you this." He pulled out a black handgun that he had been hiding behind him.

He waved it around at her for a few seconds then put his face right up to hers. Alex tried to turn away from him, but he was quick, and he grabbed her with his left hand, turning her face back into his. She could smell his breath, cigarettes and whiskey, and she whimpered.

"I said, take your FUCKING CLOTHES OFF, NOW!"

As he screamed his spittle hit her face, and she blinked to keep it from hitting her in the eyes. His hand grew tighter still on her face, and all of a sudden he was shoving her with his free arm up against the wall. Her head hit the plexiglass with a thud. She cried out in pain, and he laughed. He held her there against the wall and stared at her, stared into her soul. Her heart was beating so fast now she couldn't tell if there were any pauses between beats anymore. It seemed as if it had just become one frantic, humming beat. Why? Why? Why? Her voice screamed in her head.

He looked at her for a second, his desire palpable. He turned her face to the left and licked her. His tongue was hot, and he moved it from her collarbone up to her ear. He grew more excited when he felt her shake all over. She was sobbing now, and he loved the sounds she made. She felt his breath on her ear.

"I will ask you one more time, and then I will not ask you anymore," he whispered in her ear. "Please, *take off your fucking clothes, now!*"

Alex knew she would have to do what he said this time. She tried to nod, but his hand was so strong, so paralyzing. She managed to whisper an audible "okay" to him. He released his steely grip on her, and she fell to the floor. He stood over her and when she looked up, she could see the bulge in his pants, wanting her. Her heart sank. She knew what was about to happen, and she was powerless to stop it. If she fought, he would probably kill her. The only way she could stay alive at this point was by doing what he demanded.

She stood up on wobbly legs and began to remove her top layer of clothes. He watched her intently. She paused after removing the first layer until he lifted the gun and motioned for her to continue. She looked away from him, sighed, and began to remove her own sweat-shirt. She bent over and took off her running pants. She stopped to look at him once she was down to her sports bra and panties. She shivered in the cold room. The battery lamp flickered on the desk. She took off her panties and bra. When she did, she saw a shift in his eyes, something burning deep inside the holes of his face.

Alex knew she could not stop him. He was too far gone. His black eyes started to glaze over, and his veins were popping out of his neck. She stood, shaking from head to toe, and just hoped it would all be over soon. She turned her face away from him. She didn't want to give him the pleasure of seeing her cry.

"Turn around," he demanded.

Oh, god, she thought. *Please, no.* But she turned around and gave her back to him. She could feel his eyes all over her body, burning holes into her flesh. She could hear him moving behind her, the rustling of clothes, his breath rapid, panting. She stood, not wanting to move, yet wanting to run, run as far as she could, to get away from him. She needed to put herself somewhere else, into another time and place. She needed to be someone else right now. Suddenly she felt his hot breath on the back of her neck. *Oh, god,* she thought.

"Get down on your knees," he sneered into her neck.

The skin on her body crawled with disgust everywhere, like bugs, crawling, marching, moving. This time she vomited into her mouth, and she had to put up her hand to keep it from coming out. She turned to her left and wretched onto the concrete floor. He laughed at her then, a wicked, deep laugh.

"Get on your knees, Alex," he said, with urgency this time.

Alex knew the urgency. He desired her, and he was going to take her, whether she wanted him to or not. She swallowed deeply and, again, tried to put herself somewhere else. She closed her eyes and lowered herself to the floor. The concrete was frozen and hard on her knees.

She knelt in front of him, and he immediately had his hands all over her body. He touched her all over, rubbing her back, her buttocks, her shoulders, lightly at first, then harder. He grabbed her arms, pulled them up over her head, and told her to hold them there. Her body was frozen from the cold and fright. He grabbed at her breasts and belly, his hands racing over her like a hungry animal playing with its prey. She could feel the heat coming off of his body, but it did nothing to warm her up. She closed her eyes and held them shut so tightly that they began to burn. Suddenly, she felt him shove her from the back, and she fell forward, her palms hitting the concrete floor. She winced as the concrete dug into her skin and, before she knew it, he was grabbing at her inner thighs, forcing them apart. She cried out again, this time pleading.

"Please, Bobby, you don't have to do this. Please, you're hurting me."

He laughed again. This time his laugh was high pitched as if it came from someone completely different. It was filled with anger, lust, and something else...something she had never heard before and hoped she would never hear again. Her knees scraped against the floor with the movement, and she knew they were bleeding. He was grunting behind her, guttural and animalistic.

Suddenly, he was inside her. The burning was like nothing she had ever felt before. Pain engulfed her. She screamed. He laughed. She screamed again. He moaned. He moved behind her, thrusting himself inside her. *Oh, my God, the pain*, she screamed inside her head. It was the dream. The monster was here, behind her, chasing her. She could feel his breath on her back. She couldn't stop the pain inside her, something thrusting, cutting, and ripping her open. She screamed again. Run, mija, run! She could hear Abuela screaming inside her head. I can't, she screamed back. Faster, the pain came harder and faster, and she could hear the monster screaming. He moved above her, strong, evil, death behind her. *Please, kill me*, she thought. He had his hands on her sides, his fingertips digging into her hip bones. He pushed himself into her until she thought he might explode right through her stomach. *Oh, God, Dios mio*. Her insides were being torn apart. *Help me. Help me. Help me. Oh, God, please, help me.* The monster screamed in pleasure, and something hot came, boiling, fluid inside her, burning her insides. *The fires of hell*, she thought. *Oh, God, please.* Alex felt one last thrust from the monster and then nothing else. The world went black.

CHAPTER FORTY-TWO

BOBBY WALKED DOWN THE DARK HALL WHISTLING TO himself, carrying a near empty bottle of whiskey, and puffing on an almost dead Camel cigarette. He dropped the smoke and jammed the heel of his boot into it, tattooing ash into the concrete floor. He examined the whiskey bottle momentarily, then swigged the remainder of the amber liquid before chucking the bottle at one of the empty cubicles. He chuckled as the glass shattered on impact, then licked his lips as an afterthought and dug into his pocket, rummaging for the key. He felt his stomach flip at the same time he heard the lock click.

The heavy metal door banged shut behind him, and he walked over to where Alex lay. She appeared to be sleeping, her body small under the blankets, the rhythmic rise and fall of breathing barely visible in the dim light of the battery lamp. He watched her for a moment, hearing his own breath, heavy with excitement.

"Hello, Alex," he called.

He could hear his voice echo slightly in the room, and he barely recognized it.

"I know you're awake. Why don't you turn over and let me have a look at you," he enticed.

When she didn't move Bobby reached out and touched her shoulder, eliciting a sad sounding "No!" from the blankets.

"Hey, hey now, I am not going to hurt you," he said, trying to soothe her.

Bobby jumped slightly when Alex turned on him like a rabid animal, eyes wild with fear and anger. She scurried backwards on all fours until her back hit the wall as she tried to escape him. Bobby smiled at her, encouragingly.

"Oh honey, please don't back away from me. You don't have to worry. I wouldn't hurt you. I want to *enjoy* you. And I want to enjoy our time together."

He smiled again reaching out for her, but she shrank away from him as if he was a leper. Bobby could feel the anger rising in him. How dare she act this way! He could feel his face growing warm and his heart pounding faster.

"So, you want to be that way, huh? You know…" Bobby sucked a sharp breath in and stopped.

Calm down or you are going to do something you are going to regret. If you kill her now, you will have done it all for nothing, he thought to himself. He took in another deep breath and collected himself.

"I have been watching you for a while. I know that you are alone, and that you must be lonely. I only want to fill that void. I just want to be near you," he trailed off.

He didn't realize how much he had grown to desire her until he said it out loud. Now, standing there in front of her, he felt vulnerable and afraid of rejection, as he had so many years ago.

She is going to reject you, just like the first one. They are just alike. They are all the same. Just fuck her and kill her. Take her body

and her breath. Bobby smiled at Alex again, but this time the warmth was gone.

"Stand up!" he demanded.

He waited, but Alex didn't move.

"I said, STAND UP!" Bobby yelled.

He could see her flinch when he yelled at her and watched as she stood up, shaking all over. He grew excited to see her like this. Tears were beginning to roll down her face, and they glistened in the low glow of the lamp. Bobby looked Alex up and down. He had waited so long to have her in front of him. *God, how long I have waited for you. I didn't think I would ever see you again.*

"What the hell do you want from me?" she screamed.

She was furious and scared, wet with sweat and tears, and the sight of her sent him into a tailspin. He grew instantly hard, and he thought he could climax just watching her.

"Take off your clothes..." he whispered.

"What?" she looked confused.

"I said take…. off….. your….. clothes."

Bobby didn't have time for any more games. He raised his voice and made sure he said each word carefully and forcefully so that Alex would not mistake him. He could see her lips trembling, and when she bit them she drew blood. His body was overheating from anticipation, sweat beads dripping down his back and face. When she still didn't move to take off her clothes, Bobby had enough.

"Oh, yeah, I forgot to show you this," he sneered.

Bobby pulled out the black handgun he had stuffed in his back pocket. He waved it around a few times, then put his sweaty cheek right up against Alex's. She tried to turn away, but Bobby grabbed her chin with his free hand and turned her to face him.

"I said take your FUCKING CLOTHES OFF, NOW!" he screamed in her face.

Bobby's desire and rage were near the boiling point. He could feel the sting of a million fire ants inside his skin as the mixture of frustration and desire swallowed him whole. He shoved Alex with his free arm up against the wall, hitting her head against the plexiglass with a thud. She cried out.

"*Ha, ha, ha,*" the evil laughed out loud through Bobby's mouth. ***Hold her, boy. Show her who the man is. She is just a whore. She's gonna give it to you, give it to you good.*** Bobby held Alex against the wall, staring at her scared helpless face. Then he turned that fear away from him and licked her neck. He could taste the sweat, the fear, the anger, and it elated him. Her body shook and his followed. Hers with fear, his with excitement.

"I will ask you one more time, and then I will not ask you anymore," he whispered in her ear. "Please, take off your fucking clothes, now!"

She choked out a whimper of agreement, and he released her. Alex fell to the floor, and Bobby stepped back a bit so he could watch her. He stared as she again stood on shaky legs and started to slowly remove the top layer of clothing she wore. She stopped. *What are you doing? No, no, honey.* Bobby urged her to continue with the shiny metal of the gun. She reluctantly removed her sweatshirt and pants, then stopped to look at him, shivering in her sports bra and panties. After a moment, she stripped off the rest of her clothing, baring all for him to see.

My God, did she know how beautiful she was? The lamp cast a glow on her, a halo. *She's an angel.* Her body was perfect. Her breasts were full, and and her hips curvy. Her face was soaked with tears that glistened in the light. His heart pounded in his chest and ears. He felt another pounding between his thighs, so forceful it reverberated through his entire body.

Take her now, you fucking idiot. This is what you have been waiting for. This is what you have risked your life for. This is what you have worked so hard for. All of it. So take her already.

He wanted her so badly, but he knew he could not have her and not take her life if he was not careful. He could not face her. He could not see her face.

"Turn around," Bobby told her.

He could see the fear in her eyes grow as they widened even more. She paused for a moment but then slowly turned her back to him. *God, her back is just as beautiful. I knew all that running would make her legs strong and shapely. I have to have her.* Bobby moved closer to her until he could feel the warmth of his breath return to him from the back of her neck.

"Get down on your knees," he hissed.

Bobby barely recognized his voice. It came from somewhere else. He knew it came out of his mouth, yet it came from somewhere else. Suddenly Alex vomited on the floor, and from that same alien place, Bobby heard a guttural laugh emerge from his gaping mouth.

"Get on your knees, Alex!" he demanded, urgency soaking every word.

She barely hit the floor before he had his hands all over her, touching her body and hair, grabbing at her breasts and buttocks, feeling her cold skin under his hot hands. He pulled her hands up over her head and demanded she keep them there so he could get a better look at her. Bobby stood and ripped at his clothes, pulling his pants down as fast as he could, sweat dripping down his face. He knelt down behind her and shoved her forward, grabbing at her waist, not hearing her cry out in pain. A rush of sound filled his head, a tornado of wind blaring in his ears, blocking out the world. Then all he could hear was the evil.

Now, boy! Do it now. Take her like you took her so many times before. She is yours. You have waited so long. This is your moment. You can do whatever you want to her, with her. She is yours. All yours. Do it. Do it, now.

Bobby entered her, and the room spun around him. He thrust inside her, deep and hard, reveling in the feeling of her. She was perfect. She was everything he remembered. Oh, how he had missed her. He thrust harder and harder, digging his fingernails into Alex's hips, until he could wait no longer. Bobby exploded with pleasure inside of her.

"Oh, Angela, my sweet love….." he whispered.

CHAPTER FORTY-THREE

MANNY AND DESHAWN SAT AT THEIR DESKS, FACING ONE another, looking over the files on Bobby Benson, Jr., again and again. Phone call after phone call poured into the station throughout the day regarding Alex and Bobby. Most were just sharks with no real information...just looking for reward money. *Reward money makes people say crazy things*, Manny thought. The police precinct buzzed with nervous energy as uniforms raced against the clock to collect information regarding any tips that came in. Their window of the initial forty-eight hours was fast approaching.

The connection between the young girl, Amanda, and the fact that she worked at the cafe where Alex stopped every morning, hadn't surprised them. The family had come in to identify the body. Manny sat thinking again, for at least the hundredth time in his career, how difficult it must be as a parent to have to bury your child, especially for something like this. Amanda was so young. He had accompanied the family to the morgue and couldn't help but share in their grief, although his was for Alex.

After Amanda's family left, Manny and Deshawn went over to the cafe to gather any information they could. Thankfully, it was still early morning, and they would see most of the regulars. It was a quick ride there, and a silent one, each detective deep in thought. It wasn't until Manny was pulling into the parking lot of the cafe that either spoke.

"Hey, man, you know we are gonna get this bastard, right?" Deshawn turned to Manny, his face earnest.

Manny looked at his partner and friend. He was grateful for the caring words at that moment, and he managed a half smile. *Yeah, man, I am hoping with my entire heart and soul. You have absolutely no idea.*

"Yeah, buddy. I know we are. He's gonna wish he never even stepped foot in our town. Now let's go get us some info," Manny said, tapping Deshawn's notepad that he held absentmindedly.

The cafe smelled of freshly ground dark roasted coffee beans and toasted bread. The chatter of morning breakfast eaters and clinking of tea cups and stirring spoons filled the room. Manny stopped for a moment and took it all in, imagining Alex starting her morning here every day. He took a deep breath and filled his lungs with the glorious smells, which elicited a small growl from his stomach.

"Deshawn, you take Bobby's mug around, and I will find the manager," Manny said.

Deshawn nodded and waded into the tightly packed tables while Manny stood in the ordering line. A few moments later a pimply faced kid with glasses looked up at him with mild curiosity and what might have been construed as moderate disdain.

"Can I help you?" he asked.

"Yes, you can. My name is Detective Castillo, and I need to see your manager."

The kid's mouth dropped open slightly. He stood still for a moment, as if he didn't quite understand what Manny had said to him. Manny waited a moment. Sometimes this happened when people were confronted with law enforcement, they just froze for a second. Sometimes it was due to their own infractions, sometimes just some strange fear or anxiety. Manny had gotten used to it over the years. He would wait patiently for a moment, and if it took too long or he was running short of patience, he would "nudge" them. Unfortunately, this kid seemed to be a little on the "stuck" end, and Manny was definitely short on patience right now.

"Hey, kid!" Manny urged.

"Oh, yeah, right, hold on," he said as he turned and headed to a back room.

After a few moments, the manager came from out back with the young kid with the pimply face following behind him. Manny told the manager why they were there and showed him pictures of both Alex and Bobby. The boy told Manny that he had seen Alex the morning of her abduction, and that she had ordered coffee.

"Wait, are you sure she came in at 5 a.m.?" Manny asked, surprised.

"Yeah, I'm sure," the kid retorted, annoyed.

Manny thought for a moment. Alex didn't usually go running until five. If she had come in at five, she either hadn't gone running, or she had gone an hour earlier than her normal routine. It ate away at him not knowing why she had deviated from her routine. He was so angry with himself that he hadn't put up more of a fight when she had told him to go home.

"Do you remember what she was wearing?" Manny asked.

"Um, man, I don't know," the kid scoffed.

The manager looked at him and elbowed the kid.

"Ouch, Dad, come on…" he whined.

"Try to remember, Trevor. This is very important," the manager, Trevor's dad, urged.

"Okay, um, she was wearing…" he paused thinking for a moment. "She was wearing some winter running pants and big sweatshirt, and a skully cap and scarf, and maybe some gloves, I think. She was that lady who kept asking me all those questions about Amanda. She was annoying," Trevor added.

Trevor's dad elbowed him again, provoking another whine from his son's mouth. The father and son looked at one another, holding each other's gaze in some kind of unspoken stand-off. Manny waited for a moment, but again grew impatient. *I don't have time for this crap.*

"So she was alone when she came in, and she left alone?" he prodded.

"Yes," Trevor said.

"Was this guy here that day?" Manny asked, showing him the picture of Bobby again.

"I don't think so," Trevor said. "I'm not totally sure, though. I was super tired, ya know? I am not used to working the morning shift. Here I am again, though, working the morning shift," Trevor complained.

Man, this kid is a whiny shit, Manny thought. He took in a deep breath and tried to calm himself a bit. He was slowly losing his temper. He was running out of time. Deshawn rejoined him just then, nodding at him.

"Okay, well thank you both for your cooperation. Here is my card in case you can think of anything else. Please, give me a call," Manny said, shoving his card into the manager's hand.

Shortly after they returned to the office, Manny got a phone call from the lab, confirming what he already knew deep down. The fingerprints on the coffee cup, left at what was now being considered the abduction site, were Alex's. Manny had over half of the Deployment Team back over to the area within fifteen minutes of receiving the phone call. A lot of the time, killers will have certain patterns and usually keep their victims somewhat close to where they live or where they were abducted. Sometimes they fled and actually left the state, or in a few cases, the country. But Manny had a feeling in the pit of his stomach that Alex was close, and that she was still alive. He could feel her.

"You okay?" Deshawn asked him, pulling Manny from his thoughts.

"Yeah, it is just getting late," Manny answered quietly, rubbing his temples.

Deshawn knew what he meant by "getting late." Manny didn't mean the time. He meant it was almost forty-eight hours since Alex had gone missing. Manny's eyes were dark and sad. The black circles under them had grown darker and had set themselves deeper into the flesh, threatening to remain a permanent feature. Deshawn was very concerned about him. They sat across from each other, shuffling through the papers on their desks, trying to pass the time without going stir crazy. Deshawn could feel the tension surrounding Manny and thought he looked like he was about to jump out of his skin.

"You wanna go out and ride the streets for a while?" Deshawn asked.

"I don't know. It's almost midnight, and there's at least seven inches of snow out there. I think I will just hang here and see if any more information comes in. But you should probably get back to your family. Muriel will be waiting up for you," Manny answered, trying to smile.

"Man, you're gonna make me leave you here again? Why don't you let me drive you home for the night? We can get up at the ass crack of dawn again and come back in," Deshawn coaxed.

Manny gave him a look that hung on the edge of frustration. Deshawn snorted at him, already aware of what was coming next.

"Deshawn, I shouldn't have to remind you that we are coming up on forty-eight hours really quickly here and...." Manny's voice trailed off, as if someone had turned the volume down on him.

Deshawn knew why. Manny didn't want to finish his sentence for a reason. They all knew that the first forty-eight hours were imperative in a crime, whether it be in finding the victim alive, or finding all the clues from the murder victim in order to find their suspect in time. Many times, if forty-eight hours had gone by, it became much less likely to find a kidnapped victim alive, and harder to find a murder suspect. Deshawn sighed and looked away from Manny. He stared out the window and watched as the snowflakes fell fast and heavy. They sat together in silence for what seemed like an eternity, neither speaking, while the roar of the other detectives' phones, voices, and t.v.'s blared all around them.

"Alright." Deshawn finally gave in to their silent stand off. "I am going to go home then. At least give me the key to your apartment so that I can stop by in the morning and get you some clean clothes and shit," Deshawn insisted.

Manny sighed and dug into his coat pocket, producing the keys to his place. He held them out for Deshawn to take. Deshawn looked at him for a few seconds before grabbing the keys and winking at Manny.

"Do us all a favor and go into the lounge and get a few hours sleep on the couch in there, even though it is uncomfortable as hell," Deshawn said. Then he turned, defeated, and walked away.

Manny watched as he left the office. He knew Deshawn meant well and was only looking out for him, but Manny was not willing to sleep until he knew Alex was safe. He knew she was out there, and it was killing him that he didn't know where. It was eating at him that he couldn't just run out and save her, that he couldn't protect her. All he could do was sit idly by and wait for someone to drop something into his lap.

He hadn't prayed in a long time. He hadn't been to church since he was a teenager and his mother had made him go. She was a devout Catholic, and she tried to raise Manny to be the same. He had grown to despise the deeper, darker things that had come to light about the Catholic church, namely some of the Priests that had been outed in the last few years. It wasn't just that thought, though. In his line of work, he had begun to question if there truly was a God anyway, with all the evil he had seen since the start of his career. But in that moment, he was at a loss for anything else to do. He closed his eyes and folded his hands. He laid his head on top of his hands and, right there at his desk in front of anyone that might be paying attention, he prayed. *Oh, God,* he prayed silently, *please help me, please help me, Father. Our father, who art in heaven, hallowed be thy name……*

CHAPTER FORTY-FOUR

ALEX LAY QUIETLY, THE ONLY SOUND IN THE ROOM THE raspy breath in her own dry throat. Her body shuddered with each breath, pain flooding her with each new emotion as it reared its ugly head again and again…. hate, fear, agony, defeat, remorse… *Why didn't I fight him? Why didn't he kill me?* Each thought stabbed at her with the sting of silence that followed.

The battery lamp cast an eerie glow around the room, throwing shadows upon the walls. Dancing demons that played tricks with her mind, beckoning her. *This is hell,* she thought. *I really did die, and I have been cast to hell. Or worse, this is purgatory.* The burning pain seized her body again. She couldn't even utter an audible cry anymore. Her voice was gone, her will nothing more than a shell of what it had been.

If I'm not truly dead, I am going to die, she thought. She moved slightly and noticed dampness between her legs. She was shocked for a moment, embarrassed that she had urinated on herself at some point. She pushed back the blankets and gasped when she saw the pool of blood on the mattress and between her legs. She also hadn't realized she was still completely naked.

Bobby had raped her five or six times during the time he was with her. She wasn't sure how long he had stayed. He had punched her a few times, but she didn't think anything was broken. He had apologized over and over, saying he didn't want to hurt her pretty face. Alex remembered very little, thankfully, slipping in and out of consciousness for most of the ordeal. Her body felt as if it had been raked over hot coals. The pain was immense. She had been helping Manny for a while now, providing input on different violent cases for the police. She had seen her share of what many would call "crazies," and heard many stories of the victims they had tortured, beaten, raped, and killed. But she herself had never been a victim until now. *How ironic to be on the other side.* She always had empathy, even unable to hold back tears at times...at crime scenes or with victims' families. But she knew she would never be the same after this.

That is, if I live through this, she thought morbidly.

Bobby had left her some time ago, promising to return. The thought caused her to shudder involuntarily, and she belched a dry heave forceful enough to make her head spin. Alex panicked a moment, wondering if she had only dreamt that he left, and scanned the room like a wild animal searching for it's hunter. Thankfully, he was nowhere to be found.

Okay, Alex, pull it together! You've seen all kinds of victims. Now you are a victim. What did the other victims have that you don't? Yes, girl... Death! Alex coached and reassured herself. She knew if she didn't pull herself together post haste, she would soon join the ranks of the Grafton Hill Strangler's body count. She had to think. How much time did she have? Her sense of time was so obscured in here.... *Think, think, come on, Alex, think....*

She knew she at least needed to try and clean herself up. She struggled to sit up. Every muscle, every tendon, every inch of skin on her body ached beyond comprehension. She tried to stand and fell back, crying out like a wounded animal. *Oh, my God, what did he do to me?* she thought.

Come on, mija. Get up! she heard Abuela encourage strongly from somewhere in the distance.

Alex stood this time, landing on legs reminiscent of coming off a boat that had been on very choppy water. They felt like jello below her, not the strong runners legs of before. She slowly walked over to the cooler and took out a few bottled waters. She removed an old tattered shirt from the clothing bag he had left her. She methodically poured water onto the shirt and began wiping herself, first between her thighs. The sting surprised her making her wince, but she kept rubbing the raw flesh clean. Everything burned and ached, but she kept cleaning herself...she had to. After what seemed like hours, she was as clean as she thought she could get and began to dress herself. Her body was heavy as if it had been filled with concrete. It was so difficult to move, to do such menial tasks. Yet, she willed herself on. After some time, and a lot of energy she couldn't spare, she was dressed and had eaten a little, although it was a forced feeding.

Alex shuffled over to the dilapidated chair and eased herself into it. She looked around, really looked around this time. She surveyed the room with fresh eyes, taking her time to look at each detail with meticulous eyes. Everything seemed to look different, clearer, more threatening than before. A broken desk, the busted chair in which she sat, a locked metal door, useless blankets, a makeshift toilet, a battery operated lamp. Alex pondered her options for awhile and began to formulate a plan in her mind. After a few moments, her eyes fell on something she had not noticed before. She stood, this time on sturdier legs and walked over to the object. Alex bent to pick it up. Just as she began to formulate a plan in her mind, she jumped at the sound of the key in the lock…....

CHAPTER FORTY-FIVE

MANNY AND DESHAWN SPED DOWN THE HIGHWAY. THE cars blurred past them while the sleet pelted the windshield, ticking down the seconds in the race they were running. The tension and excitement that filled the car's interior was so palpable it threatened to smother them at any minute.

"I can't believe this shit!" Manny's voice sliced the air.

Deshawn recoiled in surprise. His smile was tentative, but hopeful. He and Manny were at the station just minutes before, again going over what little information they had on Bobby Benson when, by some luck or grace of God, they caught a break in the case. Some guy claiming his aunt and uncle rented their basement apartment to the "freak" on television called in to the station. The caller said his name was Mike something or other, and could they please hurry up because he didn't want "the crazy guy hurting my elderly aunt and uncle."

Manny's foot grew heavier on the gas pedal as he rounded the last corner, nearly fishtailing the Mustang on the slick ground. Deshawn held on to the door handle, but kept his mouth shut. He was too focused on the fact that they were nearly there and, he knew if he was this focused, Manny was ten times more focused. As if hearing Deshawn's thoughts, Manny glanced at him briefly, nodded, and returned his eyes to the road.

Oh Alex, Manny thought, *this guy has been under our noses this whole time. I'm so sorry, honey. I'm coming. Hold on.* Manny brought the car to a skidding halt and lept out before Deshawn knew the car was in park. Deshawn had to move quickly to keep up. The guy Mike, who was nothing more than a twenty-something, punk looking kid, stood by his car waiting for the detectives, keeping his distance from the apartment building. The kid started to walk towards them, and Manny drew his gun. Deshawn followed suit.

"Hey, hey…" the kid protested, his eyes wide. "I am not the bad guy!!" His voice was pitched high as if someone had kicked him between his legs.

"Shhhhhh..." Manny hissed between gritted teeth, motioning to the kid with his hand to keep his voice down. "Do you have keys to the place?"

"Ya, man, I do. But I don't think you'll need those," he whined as he pointed to the black nine millimeters in Manny and Deshawn's hands. "I don't think he's home. His black car isn't here."

Manny's heart sank into the pit of his stomach. He had been hoping to catch Bobby here, off guard. *If he isn't keeping her here, then where?* Manny's head was spinning. His heart pounded in his chest.

"Give me the keys, dammit!" Manny growled.

The kid reached out a shaky hand, and Manny ripped the keys from it.

"Ouch, man!" the kid protested.

Manny glared at him and quickly ran down the five steps to the basement door. Deshawn tried to get his attention quietly, but Manny was deaf and blind to anything but the entrance to the basement right now. When he reached the cold metal door, Manny stopped and seemed to stutter step a moment. Deshawn sighed in relief when he realized Manny had caught himself and thought twice before barging into the apartment full throttle alone. Manny looked back at Deshawn and beckoned him towards where he stood. Manny made a signal for Deshawn to move nice and quietly. Deshawn shook his head in disapproval, but slipped quietly down the stairs and took his place next to the door, facing Manny. Manny took the key and unlocked the door as swiftly and quietly as possible, letting himself and Deshawn into the apartment.

"Police! Police!" Manny yelled out as soon as they entered, waving his flashlight and weapon around the apartment.

Deshawn quickly found the light switch and bright light exploded around them, blinding them both momentarily. Manny jumped from the unexpected exposure, unsure if he was more relieved or more afraid when they found the room empty.

"Fuck!" Manny yelled as Deshawn came out of the bathroom shaking his head.

"All clear," Deshawn confirmed.

Manny stood in angry silence for a moment, contemplating his next move. Deshawn was seconds away from asking him what the plan was when a look of decision crossed Manny's face.

"Whoah, whoah Manny don't you wanna wait for the judge?" Deshawn cautioned.

Manny's body stiffened momentarily then he began to move quickly but methodically around the room in silence, picking up papers, opening drawers, lifting up the blankets on the bed, searching. Deshawn sighed. Manny flipped the mattress over, catching a glimpse of a book out of the corner of his eye. It was a photo album, laying on the box spring near an old tattered hole in the cheap material, that leaked out yellowed foam and rusty metal springs. The book was brown and aged;

the once white pages that held photo memories yellowed from years of exposure to humidity and cigarette smoke.

"Hey, man! Don't you guys need a warrant or some kinda shit like that?" the kid asked from the doorway. He had slinked his way down to the apartment once he knew it was safe.

Deshawn gave him a look that could have melted his skin instantly if things like that could happen in real life. The kid looked from Deshawn to Manny, and back to Deshawn, then sulked out of the apartment and back up the stairs. Deshawn shook his head in disbelief.

"Hey, Deshawn, look at this," Manny called, holding open the photo album.

Stuffed into the front of the photo album were loose photos of Alex, along with newspaper clippings. Manny's stomach lurched into his throat. The idea that this psycho had been close enough to Alex to take pictures of her was bad enough, but even worse was that he had done it on more than one occasion. *This crazy motherfucker had been stalking her.....*

A photo slipped out of the pile of pictures and clippings and floated to the floor. It landed face up, and Manny recognized it immediately. It was the photo of Manny and Alex that had gone missing from the fridge at her house. But Manny's face was completely scratched out. Manny's hands began to shake, and his lower lip trembled.

"Manny….." Deshawn slowly peeled the album out of Manny's hands and ushered him to a chair that stood next to a small, worn table. An empty bottle of Jameson's whiskey kept an overflowing ashtray company on the tabletop. Manny slumped at the table, whispering something inaudible to Deshawn under his breath.

Deshawn thumbed quickly through the photo album past the pictures and articles of Alex. *There's gotta be something, something else, anything.....* he thought. He found a few black and white photos, one of a farm, another of a big burly man who looked a lot like Bobby but bigger. Deshawn thought it looked a lot like a younger version of Bobby, Sr. A certified copy of a birth certificate for Robert Benson, Jr. followed, on which some of the smallest baby footprints Deshawn had ever seen were printed. *Well, now there really is no doubt who we are dealing with then,* he thought. Now they just had to find him...and Alex. As Deshawn went to turn to the next page, he lost his grip on the back of the photo album and it flipped, splaying open all the pages. Papers came floating out from the album and settled onto the dusty floor like large, square snowflakes settling onto cold concrete. Deshawn bent to pick up the papers and noticed what appeared to be a folded set of blueprints or schematics. He opened it up. His eyes floated over the floor plan of what appeared to be some kind of building. Deshawn scanned the entire paper and ended up at the far right corner where a small name stamp had been placed. Part of it had been ripped off, but enough of it remained so that Deshawn could just make out the first part. *Sterling.... Sterling....*

"Sterling!" Deshawn shouted, his voice reverberating in the small basement studio apartment and scaring Manny a little. "Sterling what?"

Manny jumped up with a start.

"The railroad!" Manny yelled at Deshawn as he took off running.

Dehawn followed closely behind. They ran to the car, leaving the basement door to the apartment wide open, the keys dangling in the lock. Manny revved the engine and reversed the Mustang like a professional Nascar driver, forgetting about the slick roads. Deshawn seemed not to notice when the car skipped a moment before grabbing salted asphalt.

"The railroad!" Deshawn repeated. "These are the original blueprints for the foreman's office and the storage facilities for the railway. There's a small building down there where the foreman used to oversee all the comings and goings of the freight that came in and out of town. The trains used to stop near there at the train depot to load and unload cargo, then it was brought over here," Deshawn said, pointing to the blueprints of the storage yard. There have to be a ton of old empty containers down there. It's like a dump yard for those things now."

Deshawn's eyes were bright with excitement. Manny's voice echoed that excitement when he looked at Deshawn and smiled. "Put on your seat belt, Freeman…. You're gonna need it!"

The squeak of the Mustang's tires when Manny put her into drive sliced through the otherwise quiet night, sending a shiver down the spine of the apartment owners' nephew as he hid in his car. He watched the tail lights disappear into the darkness.

CHAPTER FORTY-SIX

"HELLO, ALEX." BOBBY SMILED.

Alex shivered at the sound of his voice and instinctively folded herself as far into the old chair as possible, away from him. He smiled at her again, the wolf baring his teeth to his prey. She had to get out of here, no matter what it took. *Stay calm,* she willed herself. *Keep your head on straight. It is the only way.*

Bobby stepped towards her, and Alex had to use all of her will to keep herself from flinching. His smile repulsed her. He stopped a foot away and looked down upon her, a mixture of pity and lust painted on his face. Her heart raced, and her breath quickened, but she had to remain calm.

"Hi, Alex," he whispered.

She had to do it. She had to...she had no choice. *You have to do it, you don't have anymore time, and no other choice....*

"H-h-hi," Alex stammered.

Alex had to summon every fiber of her being to enable herself to face him, to speak to him, to look at him. She had to try and connect with him somehow. It was her only chance. Even though it went against every single primal instinct she was feeling, she knew it was the only thing that could buy her some time.

To her surprise, Bobby reacted. He jumped at the sound of her voice. Shock flashed momentarily across his face, but was quickly replaced with…what was it? Happiness? She prayed it was.

"Hi, Bobby," Alex managed again.

She barely recognized her own voice. It was deeper and raspier, like that of a veteran smoker. Bobby stood, towering above her. She knew she would have to get closer to him, but she was having a hard time willing her legs to move. He continued to stare at her, waiting, watching.

"I, um, I was waiting for you."

Alex managed a small smile and cleared her throat. Bobby's eyes were glued to her face. He was examining her, and Alex knew it. She had to get this just right. She had never been in drama club or theater, but she knew she better make this an award winning performance. Suddenly, Bobby chuckled awkwardly, and Alex thought he might be blushing. It was hard to tell in the dim light of the battery lamp. He inhaled deeply, and his exhale trembled. Alex knew this was it. This was her chance.

"I think we got off on the wrong foot, so to speak. I, uh, well, you took me by surprise, you see. Ya know, grabbing me like that and all." She smiled at him again, managing to stand this time.

Now they were standing close, so close she could feel his breath quicken, hot against her forehead. He was looking down at her, looming above her. It took all of her strength to turn her face up to look at him, and when she did, she locked eyes with him. How would this go? How could she do it? Would he even believe her? Alex took one trembling hand and laid it gently on his chest. She could feel his heart racing, and he sucked in a breath, as if her touch had seared his skin.

"Alex," he whispered.

His chest was hard and muscular under her fingertips. She moved them to the buttons on his shirt and traced the middle button with one single fingertip. He held his breath for a moment then let it out, this time unable to conceal the shakiness. She looked up at him and began to speak the words she had rehearsed in her mind.

"I was wondering if we could, well, maybe go a little slower this time? I am pretty sore from our last time together, and I was hoping that I could try to, well, I could…" Alex paused to see if what she was saying was having any effect on Bobby. He was watching her, carefully studying her, analyzing her. There was something there in his features that seemed to soften a bit, though, so she continued. "I could… help this time." Alex smiled at him coyly.

"Well, well, well, Alex." His tone was one she couldn't quite read.

Alex's stomach flipped nervously. Bobby stood for a moment longer, staring at her, his eyes bearing down upon her.

"What has gotten into you?" he asked, one eyebrow raised inquisitively.

"Hmmm…" She managed a small giggle. "I had a lot of time to think in this cold room all alone after you left Bobby and, call it what you want, I guess I had a change of heart."

Alex continued to trace her fingertips all around his shirt buttons. The heat coming off his body grew warmer with each passing moment, and she could feel his chest rising quicker with each breath. She knew he was becoming aroused, so she continued to talk.

"I haven't really ever had anyone care about me like you, so at first it really scared me, I'll admit it…. But I thought about it a lot, and it's kinda nice to have someone so… into me."

Alex managed to unbutton his shirt while she spoke, and she gently pushed it open to reveal his chest. His muscles bulged and rippled under his skin. She gasped at how strong he was and for a moment became ill at the thought of how difficult this was really going to be. Thankfully he mistook her gasp as a pleasurable sign, because he grabbed her arms and pulled her into him. Alex's body stiffened, and she had to remind herself that this was a matter of life and death. She loosened up and sighed audibly, trying to redeem herself. She closed her eyes and started to kiss his chest, light little kisses here and there. Bobby moaned at her touch so she continued, taking it a bit further, flicking her tongue along his skin, teasing him. His breath grew heavy, and she felt him tense. *Come on, Alex, you can do this….*

"You really…" Bobby began in almost childlike disbelief.

"Shhhhh," Alex whispered, finding his lips with one of her fingers, and they trembled as she touched them.

She touched his face, delicately tracing the scar there. His whole body shuddered, and she knew she had him. She moved back a little, taking him with her, backing up until she felt the desk behind her. *Perfect,* she thought. Bobby groped her all over, and she had to swallow the scream that welled up inside her. *Just a little more. You can do this.* She reached up and stroked his face lightly. He pulled her tighter to him, nearly squeezing the breath from her, pushing his lips onto hers.

Alex gripped him so that he wouldn't turn away. The whiskey and stale cigarettes lingered on his breath. Alex had to breathe through her nose so she wouldn't gag. She urged herself to relax. Alex could feel the urgency in his kiss and forced herself to kiss him back. She could feel his excitement growing on her abdomen, bulging excitement. Alex closed her eyes and let him touch her all over, his hands leaving behind a scorch mark wherever they roamed.

Bobby moaned, and Alex knew this was it. He kissed her more deeply, and she reached behind her as slowly as she could, feeling her way around. Her hand brushed against it, and when it did she kissed him as passionately as she could to distract him while she wrapped her fingers around the thick piece of wood. He plunged his face into her neck, and she knew she had to strike now....

CHAPTER FORTY-SEVEN

OH, MY GOD, SHE'S ACTUALLY LETTING ME. HE WAS SO aroused, he thought he might explode before he had the chance to get inside of her. She was kissing him back, her tongue dancing with his, sending shivers down his spine. At first, he couldn't believe it when she spoke to him. He wasn't sure if he was imagining it or not. Then he thought maybe she might be making fun of him or condescending to him somehow. It was the evil that made him doubt.

What are you thinking, you stupid fuck? She isn't into you! Why would she be? She is a deceitful whore.

Bobby had to find a way to shut it up. He couldn't let it control him. He couldn't let it take over. Not this time, not with her, not now. He couldn't let it force itself through this time. He wanted this one so badly. He hadn't wanted anything so badly since he was fourteen. Bobby concentrated on Alex, on her and only her. Her lips were soft, and her breasts were supple. He touched her like he knew women liked to be touched. He should have touched her this way the first time, but the evil had taken over when it saw her. He moaned and dug his face into her neck, soaking up her scent into his nostrils. *This is so amazing.*

I have waited so long for you. Bobby was smiling to himself, feeling content for the first time in a very long time, when he suddenly felt the pain. Something crashed into the side of his head, and the pain that followed was immense. It traveled from his left temple down his neck, hot searing pain that made him gasp. The world began to spin, and he grabbed at anything he could to keep himself from toppling over, but he couldn't see. *What? Wait, why can't I see?* He panicked. Blood was pouring into his eyes. Bobby screamed, partly from the pain, partly out of anger. *What the fuck?* What had hit him? The pain was almost unbearable, and he cried out again.

"Alex!" he screamed.

The world spun around him once more and then he felt it; the cold concrete smacked him on the side of his face, and then he felt nothing at all because the world went black.

CHAPTER FORTY-EIGHT

ALEX SCREAMED WHEN SHE SAW THE PIECE OF WOOD, with its long, thick nails, sticking out of Bobby's head. She stood for a moment, watching as the blood poured from him. She screamed again when she heard the sickening thud his face made as it hit the floor, like a carcass of meat being slammed onto the killing floor. Alex was frozen, unable to move, her eyes riveted to the river of blood that began to swirl around Bobby's head. He didn't move after that, and for a moment she wondered if he was dead. A flood of memories ravaged her mind, and a small cry escaped her lips. Then from somewhere far away she heard the scream...

"Run, mija, run!!!"

It was Abuela's voice. She wanted Alex to run. Alex's eyes snapped open, and it was enough to get her feet to move. She carefully negotiated around Bobby's limp body and walked as quickly as she could to the door. She prayed silently that he hadn't locked it behind him. She couldn't remember seeing him do it, but that didn't mean anything. Everything was fuzzy and felt like it happened hours ago, like an old dream that was fading in the early morning light.

Alex reached the door and had to stifle a crazed laugh when she realized it wasn't locked. She turned the handle and froze once again when she heard movement behind her. *Oh God, no. Don't look back,* she thought. She tried with all her might not to turn her head, but against her will it turned on its own, as if being controlled by someone else. There he was, looking up at her, the gash oozing blood around the rusty nails that were sunk deep into the flesh of his skull.

"Alex," his voice warned.

He sounded weaker than before, but he was definitely not dead. The scream came again, powerful, booming in her head.

"Run, Alex!! RUN, NOW!!"

Alex pulled open the heavy metal door and looked around frantically. She was in some kind of warehouse. Darkness and frigid air shrouded her. Her eyes swept back and forth, desperately looking for something familiar, when finally they fell upon an old red exit sign. *Oh God, thank you!* Alex ran.

CHAPTER FORTY-NINE

THE SUN STILL SLEPT BEHIND THE RIDGE TO THE EAST. THE sky was betwixt the dark purple of night and the pale blue of day. A gust of icy wind sliced through her, cutting off her air supply for a split second. She gasped, pulling a frozen chunk of air into her lungs. She looked around, squinting, trying to get her bearings. *Where am I?* Nothing around her was familiar. It seemed as if she had been thrown into a graveyard for monstrous metal cans, their carcasses empty and rotting with rust. She began to slowly weave her way around abandoned railway cars, her bare feet already numb from the frozen slab of ground beneath her. Alex shivered, the hair on the back of her neck erect. That's when she heard his wail break the air.

"Alex!"

His long drawn out cry was a mixture of pain and anger, and it frightened her like nothing before. Her skin crawled with urgency. Alex squinted her eyes again, scanning her surroundings, looking desperately for a place to run, a place to hide, to escape.

"I see you, you little bitch!" Bobby screamed.

Alex's feet moved. She didn't know where they were taking her, and she didn't care. She could hear his heavy footsteps fast approaching, and she pushed her legs into a run, pumping them. Alex caught a flash of light out of the corner of her eyes, but fear gripped her and kept her from looking anywhere but straight ahead.

The pale light from the approaching dawn was enough to illuminate the opening of a large dark hole that loomed before her, cut deep into the side of a rocky mound of earth. Old rusty railroad tracks were laid out like a red carpet before her, guiding her. Alex's feet tried to find their way in between the old splintered wood of the track, but she could already feel the cuts and raw lesions that were forming, her exposed soles vulnerable to the elements of her surroundings. She thought, momentarily, that she must have gone completely insane. Otherwise, she would not be running towards the black abyss of a tunnel that stood before her; yet it beckoned her, pulling her towards it, promising escape.

"I'm going to kill you, you whore!" Bobby taunted.

His voice was much closer now, and Alex could hear him running. She was too scared to look back to gauge his proximity, but by the sound, he was only a few yards behind her. She had to kick it up a notch, full throttle run. She hoped a sudden burst of speed would be enough to put some distance between them. Alex began to sprint. The tunnel's gaping mouth swallowed her, and she disappeared.

CHAPTER FIFTY

MANNY COULD BARELY BREATHE. HIS HEART WAS RACING, and his hands were clenched so tightly on the steering wheel that his knuckles blanched a pale white in stark contrast to his otherwise almond skin. His heart sank with each passing minute. *What if I am too late? What if we are running on the wrong intel? I cannot live without her!* All the "what ifs" pounded his brain, crashing against his skull like the hulking waves of an incoming tide slamming the sand.

".... little light at least." Deshawn's voice found its way through the whooshing sound in Manny's ears. "Manny?"

"Yeah, man, sorry. I just...I'm just scared that's all," Manny admitted with an unsuccessful smile.

"Nah, no worries." Deshawn gently patted Manny's shoulder. "I was just saying that at least there is a little light. I hate trying to look for things in the dark, ya know?" Deshawn sighed.

"Alex!" Manny exclaimed.

Deshawn jumped at Manny's scream. He looked at Manny staring through the passenger window and followed his gaze. The headlights flashed briefly onto a tall, thin figure just before it was enveloped by the darkness of an old train tunnel. The car headlights lingered enough to show another, much larger, figure close behind the first. The second figure moved less fluidly than the first, almost as if crippled by something. It ran with a hitch, bent forward awkwardly. Deshawn knew immediately it was Bobby Benson, Jr., as did Manny. The sense of urgency and anxiety that followed was palpable.

"Shit!" Manny yelled.

Manny floored the gas pedal of the Mustang, spewing a cloud of dirt and debris from its rear as the tires tried desperately to find traction on the gravel road. He drove towards the tunnel, switching the headlights to high beam setting.

"Okay, Castillo, we got this. Don't worry…" Deshawn coached.

"Got it," Manny answered, concentrating on his next move.

"Wait, hold up… You are gonna slow down, right? Manny, hey, Manny…" Deshawn's voice grew thick with nervous worry.

Manny gained speed as he neared the tunnel. He ran the Mustang up alongside the train tunnel and prayed there was enough room for the car to make it to the end. He also prayed that he made it in time. The car jumped and skidded over the rough terrain, pebbles pinging the undercarriage. Manny was usually so careful with his car. It was a vintage 1976 he had restored and obsessed over. Manny either didn't notice or didn't care. He stayed focused and intent on finding the exit to the massive tunnel.

"Manny….." Deshawn tried again. Silence.

Suddenly the end of the tunnel was visible. Manny whipped the Mustang around so that it's headlights were glaring into the black orifice of the tunnel. He jumped out of the car and drew his gun. He stood in front of the humming Mustang in between the headlights, squinting into the aperture of the mountain. Deshawn joined him quickly, his weapon also drawn and pointed towards the darkness. Manny looked at Deshawn.

"We should..."

Alex's scream cut him off, and they ran into the mouth of the beast.

CHAPTER FIFTY-ONE

ALEX RAN AS HARD AS SHE COULD, BUT SHE COULD TELL
he was only a few feet behind her now. She could almost feel him
breathing down her neck. Her legs and feet were burning, and her breath
caught sharply in her tight chest. She knew she didn't have much time,
and she tried to push harder, but her legs wouldn't move any faster. She
could feel the tightness, the lactic acid building up, the burning pain,
threatening to stop her all together.

"I'm going to make you suffer the way you made me suffer!"
Bobby yelled.

His voice pierced her ears and caused her to stutter step. Her
ankle turned, and she cried out as her legs buckled beneath her. Alex
fell, and he was instantly upon her. She screamed.

Alex could feel his hands on her, pulling at her clothes, his
fingers raking her skin. He was so heavy on top of her legs. She gasped
for air and looked ahead trying to get her bearings. That's when she
saw the light. It was far away but she could see it. *Oh God, oh God. I
have to get there,* she thought. She groped for something to pull herself
with and found a wooden slab, part of the train track. She gripped the

wood and tried desperately to pull herself away from his grasp. Just as she got a grip, he yanked her legs, pulling her so hard that some of her fingernails ripped back from their nail beds. Alex screamed in agony.

"Aha, you stupid bitch! I've got you now!!"

Bobby laughed hysterically as he hauled her towards him. She writhed on the ground, kicking and hitting at the air, hoping to connect to something, anything, where she might inflict pain upon him.

He was on top of her in seconds, and his weight suffocated her. She squirmed beneath him, but his body was like a stone on her chest. She could feel his hands wrap around her throat, and the pressure was immense. She tried with all the strength she had left to pull his hands from her neck, but he was too strong. Alex tried arching her back to pull some air, any air into her lungs. But nothing could make it past his grip. She could hear him laughing, harsh and high pitched all at once. His insanity was evident in its depths. Bobby's laugh started to fade with her consciousness. She wasn't breathing, and her body was shutting down. Just as she felt the last of herself fading away, she heard an explosion from far away...and then everything went black.

CHAPTER FIFTY-TWO

MANNY AND DESHAWN RAN BLINDLY DOWN THE TUNNEL as the gleam from the headlights faded more and more. They could hear them, fighting, scuffling, shouting. The pounding of Manny's heart was deafening in his ears. He needed to concentrate. *Breathe deep,* he thought. Each scream that came from Alex tore at his heart. *Why the hell is it taking so long to reach them?*

Their footsteps pounded to the beat of his heart and echoed loudly in the tunnel. Manny could hear Deshawn's breath, as heavy as his own, and knew he must be just as anxious. *This is the longest few yards of our lives,* Manny thought.

Manny raised his gun as he approached them. He could see just enough to know that the monster was on top of Alex, and he had his hands wrapped around her throat. Manny took in a deep breath, raised his gun, and, as he exhaled, pulled the trigger.

The explosion rocked the tunnel. Then another and another. The sound of gunfire perforated the stale air of the tunnel and blasted their ears, echoing through their heads and pulsing through their bodies. Manny watched as Bobby's body froze then, as if someone hit the slow motion button, fell sideways and slumped to the ground. Deshawn ran over to the body and pulled it off of Alex.

"Alex!" Manny ran to her.

Manny bent down and gathered her up into his arms. She wasn't moving, her body lifeless.

"Alex," Manny whispered. "Alex, come on, honey!" he coaxed, but she still didn't move.

Manny jumped at the sound of gunshots. Bang, bang, bang…. He looked over to see Deshawn emptying his gun into Bobby's lifeless body.

"What the…?" Manny yelled.

"Sorry, man. Just making sure this motherfucker is dead!" Deshawn said.

It was light enough in the tunnel now that Manny could see Deshawn frowning down at him and Alex, his face lined deeply with concern. Manny looked back at Alex and placed his fingertips at her neck to check for a pulse, a tear slipping down his cheek. When he felt nothing he began CPR.

CHAPTER FIFTY-THREE

ALEX COULD HEAR ABUELA FROM FAR AWAY. SHE LOOKED around for her frantically, searching everywhere. It was dark all around her, she couldn't see anything. She could only hear Abuela's voice.

"Abuela, donde estas? Where are you?" Alex cried.

"Aqui, mija. I am here, child," Abuela answered, sounding a little closer than before. Alex looked to her left and saw a dim light coming toward her.

"Abuela, is that really you?" she asked. Alex's voice sounded much younger, the voice of a child, and she cried out in fear. "Abuela, please, help me!"

"I don't need to help you, mija." The voice still sounded far away but stronger than before. "He is there, mija, waiting for you. Go to him," she urged.

"Who, Abuela? Who is there?" Alex whimpered.

"He is there, mija. He will help you." Abluela spoke kindly. Alex missed her so much. Her heart ached at the sound of her voice.

"But I want to go with you, Abuela. I belong with you!" Alex protested.

"No, it is not your time. Now go to him and finish what you are supposed to do, mija," Abuela insisted.

Her voice was more stern now, and Alex was compelled to obey her. Alex thought that if she turned away from her for a moment Abuela might forget and let her go with her. She turned her back to the light and pretended not to hear her.

"Alex! Alex!" Abuela insisted. Alex tried harder not to hear her name.

"Alex! Alex! Come on, honey! Please, baby, please!"

Something was shaking her. She was trying so hard not to listen, not to be swayed by Abuela's persistence. More shaking. *No, no, no......*

"Alex!!"

That isn't Abuela.

"Alex, honey. There are some people here to help you." Manny said softly.

Alex opened her eyes. Manny.... *"He is waiting for you"........*

CHAPTER FIFTY-FOUR

ALEX SLOWLY OPENED HER EYES. THE ROOM WAS START-ing to fill with the gentle light of dawn. She stretched and yawned. She looked up at the ceiling like she did every morning and whispered, "Good morning, Abuela."

"You okay?" a voice, gravely with sleep, asked.

Alex smiled and rolled over to greet the voice.

"How could I not be?" she mused.

"Hmmmm," he said as he studied her face.

He seemed mostly convinced by her answer and returned her smile. He gently touched her face, feeling the smooth, chestnut skin beneath his slightly rough fingertips. *She is so beautiful,* he thought, grateful to have not lost her. His finger found her lips, and he traced them softly. She smiled again and pulled herself into his side, warm and comforting. She noticed the overly careful placement of his arms and giggled.

"Oh, Manny, I'm not going to break!" she teased. He huffed at her. She giggled again.

"Sorry if I'm being a little delicate, but I did almost lose you, okay?" he retorted.

"OK, OK, I know. But it has been almost four months since it happened, and you are allowed to touch me now without fear of hurting me. I'm completely healed," Alex argued.

Manny took a deep, exasperated breath and hugged her to him, a smile spreading his lips. She craned her neck to look up at him. He had his eyes closed, and she thought of how peaceful he looked. She laid her head on his shoulder and placed her head on his chest. The soft material of his t-shirt was soothing under her skin. She lay there quietly for a while, contemplating the events of the last few months. She shuddered at the awful memories and pulled herself even closer to him. Just as her heart began to race a little, she heard a comforting sound. A soft purr came from beneath the covers, and Alex lifted them to find the crazy little kitten trying to get comfortable at her feet. She smiled and rubbed the kitten's head with her big toe. The kitten's purr grew louder and louder.

"Silly, mija!" Alex whispered.

Manny opened one eye and peered at them. They both looked at the kitten, then at each other, and burst out laughing. The kitten started at the sound and scrambled to get out from under the covers, prompting an even greater roar of laughter from Alex and Manny.

Manny's cell phone rang, cutting through their fits of laughter. He sighed and sat up to grab his phone, picking it up on the third ring. Alex crawled to the warm spot in the bed he had left and sat next to him, contently.

"Detective Castillo," he announced.

Alex watched his face as he listened to the caller on the other end. She could only assume it was Deshawn. Manny's smile began to fade as he listened. She waited patiently until he snapped the phone shut with another heavy sigh.

"Well, Detective Castillo?" she asked.

"They found the body of a male over at the Riverdale Inn. Looks like maybe he was drugged, but he was all slashed up," Manny said, as he stood up. "Sorry."

"Don't be. You didn't do it." Alex laughed. "You know as well as I do, Detective Castillo, in our line of work there is no rest for the wicked." She smiled and stood.

"Whoah, whoah, where do you think you are going?" Manny asked.

"What do you mean?" she asked, perplexed. "I'm going with you!"

"The hell you are!" he said.

Manny started to open his mouth to argue some more, and she pushed her finger gently onto his lips to quiet him.

"Look, Manny. I know you are protecting me. I know you love me, worry about me. I know you are questioning whether I can do this. Hell, after what happened to me I sometimes questioned whether I could do it again or not. But I realized that I couldn't not do it! I have to do it. I have to help others. I was lucky enough to make it out alive, but a lot of these victims are not. I feel obligated to help you find their killers, to help bring justice to these families whose loved ones are lost. I was meant to do this," Alex argued vehemently.

Manny looked at her fierce eyes and knew she meant what she said. He knew that stubborn, set look. It meant he would never win this argument. He sighed deeply, shook his head at her in disapproval, and finished putting on his sneakers. She rushed to dress herself, and smiled as he motioned for her to hurry up.

"Well, I certainly can't tell the woman I have been waiting for my entire life, who I almost lost, "no," can I?" He looked at her and smiled, half defeated, half amused, but entirely in love. "Let's go catch us some bad guys!"